HARD CORPS

PAUL MANNERING

SEVERED PRESS
HOBART TASMANIA

HARD CORPS

CHAPTER 1

I

Tracers of azure light streaked across the screen, each indicating a ship entering the spatial dimensions of the Kursk system. Primary Marsushin's sensors reviewed the incoming data, the screen filling with lines of blue. The intel received by the Helos high command had been correct: the enemy had made their move, and the expected invasion had begun.

"Transmit alert to Arculus and the Helos Command Battle Group," Marsushin said. The computer system obeyed immediately, sending priority communications through the network and sharing the incoming data with a hundred similar screens in various ops bases across the landscape of the world.

The data coming in from the satellite array in geo-stationary orbit above the planet began to break down as the first wave of incoming weapons fire set about blinding the ground forces. A moment later the comms channel came to life in the voice of the Arculus.

"Primary, how many Diorite Commonwealth ships are in the invasion fleet?"

Marushin considered for a moment. "It appears to be all of them, Arculus."

*

Erik stared blankly at the graffiti scratched into the dark metal plate over the head of the soldier facing him. *War Is Life.*

For Erik, war was the only life he knew. With the few remaining humans facing starvation on a dozen worlds, the only option was to sign up for service in a trooper unit and go where you were told and shoot whatever life form got in your way.

The ship jolted him against the harness as they entered atmosphere. He didn't know where they were, or what the reason for the invasion of this planet was, and none of that mattered. Getting paid and getting out alive—that was all that mattered. *War is Life*. Victory was life. Getting enough together to walk away at the end of whatever term his duty required. That was life.

The recycled oxygen in the ship's atmosphere tasted warm and stale. The Diorites didn't give a shit. They breathed sulfur dioxide; oxygen was toxic to them. As long as the troopers arrived ready to fight, no thought was given to their comfort.

The platoon leader, a scar-faced block of human granite called Quarry, unclipped his harness and started shouting down the length of the carrier. "All right, you shitheads. We are two minutes away from terra firma. Are you ready to fight?!"

The troopers responded with a loud "HUP!"

Quarry spat on the floor. "I can't hear you, ya bunch of piss-stinking squats! I said, are you ready to fuck some shit up?!"

The response was deafening. Erik felt the excitement building in his blood. The need to explode out of the ship sizzled in his veins. Combat drugs didn't come close to the rush of adrenaline he felt in the moments before they were unleashed.

"You are un-fucking-killable!" Quarry roared. "You are instruments of fury! You are vengeance! You are death!"

Forty human soldiers stamped their feet and howled as they strained against their harnesses.

The troop carrier swept across the landscape of the world coded Kursk Seven-A. In the holding area, an alarm sounded and the back door slid open. The harnesses released in sequence and as soon as the straps fell away, each soldier bolted for the exit, dived into the darkness, rolled to their feet, and started firing into the swarming mess of enemy forces.

Erik felt his restraints retract and he was running for the exit, running for his life, just like he always had.

II

The route from the market to the dome wall would take Erik through Calzon's territory. He still owed the squat boss for the meat ration he had scored for Mother last week. Calzon didn't tolerate over-due debts. Being snatched by one of his boys would mean a humiliating beating and a day-night cycle in the cage where everyone could see his shame.

Erik kept running, dodging past the shuffling merchants, the trash pickers, the drunken juicers with their brains half rotted on vok. The disc of bread bounced under his shirt as he ran. It wasn't like he meant to steal it. If it hadn't fallen off the table at Mek's stall at the exact moment Erik was passing, he would never have snatched it up before it hit the mud.

If Mek hadn't yelled at him, calling him thief, he wouldn't have run. He would have handed the loaf back, hoped that Mek would give him a stale crust as a reward for saving his wares. Instead, he was running for his life through the sprawling ghetto of The Mess.

Get to Noshi, he reminded himself. Noshi would hide him and would appreciate the food he shared with her. Noshi lived alone in a box on the interior dome wall. Getting there meant going through Calzon's territory and, as his train of thought reminded him as it looped around to the same grim conclusion, that would be really dangerous.

No one looked up in The Mess; there was no point. The hexagonal panels at the top of the dome were stained with soot and dust that, even if you could see through them, would show an outside clouded by sulfurous haze. Humans couldn't survive in the atmosphere of the world. The Diorites tolerated them, letting humans live under the dome in return for menial labor and a steady supply of volunteers for military service.

Lower down, water farmers scraped the constant condensation from the panels into buckets for sale to anyone with the chits. Water gathering was dangerous work and a lot of the kids who joined the wiper crews fell to their deaths.

Not for the first time in his young life, Erik wished he could fly; being able to soar above the shacks, tents, and mud, all the way to the wall would really solve his problems. He would love nothing more than to land on Noshi's ladder and surprise her with the loaf, still warm from Mek's oven.

He kept running, splashing through the churned-up mud always underfoot. The souls living in the sealed environment generated a lot of moisture—they shit and pissed it, even breathed it out. It all ended up in the streets, becoming part of the stink and the misery of The Mess.

Passing under the flickering billboard displaying the ever-present face of Governor K'zyn, Erik turned left to avoid a blockade of handcarts and the owners arguing over who had right of way. Erik didn't know if K'zyn was real; he was a Diorite and they looked nothing like humans. Their bodies were larger than an adult human, slug like, with a dense mat of dexterous feelers covering their heads. Diorites moved by pushing the dense fluid of their interiors forward and then contracting the body left behind. The sensory tentacles on their heads worked like a hundred individual arms, and each could be extended a meter or more to independently manipulate machinery or weapons.

Erik had never seen a Diorite up close. Only the bosses like Calzon could claim they had ever spoken with one directly. For everyone else, the law was handed down from the Diorites to the bosses and then to the filthy thousands sloshing around in the dripping condensation.

"Stop that kid!"

Erik's hope that his pursuers had given up the chase were dashed by the shout. He ran faster, dodging around the slow-moving people wearing ragged clothes and hats woven from corn-husk.

Changing course, he dashed up the creaking steps to the front door of a brothel. Pushing inside, he didn't stop, sidestepping the hulking security guard who reached out to grab him and slipping through the swinging door to the back room. Two rows of flimsy curtains hid only the details of the activity going on in the cots.

Like any kid born into the filth and squalor of The Mess,

Erik had no illusions about the mechanics of sex. Actual experience was where knowledge ended and mystery began for Erik. He planned to kiss Noshi, just as soon as he worked up the courage.

The back wall of the hut proved as flimsy as the front, and a hard kick knocked a hole big enough for Erik's slight form to slip through.

With a moment to breathe, Erik took his bearings. The curving wall of the dome was in sight. Getting to it should be easy. Keep moving. He started running again. No one took any notice of a kid running. Erik and the others his age worked as messengers, running everywhere all the time, all for the chance of a scrap of food or a place to rest.

Reaching the first ladder, Erik scaled the rickety scaffolding that clung like rotting moss to the curving surface of the dome's interior wall. He climbed past sleeping platforms, smoldering cooking fires, and stinking buckets of communal waste waiting to be collected for the farmers to fertilize the crop circles on the other side of the dome.

He carefully stepped onto the narrow walkway that led to Noshi's pad. She kept it flimsy on purpose—if anyone too big for her to handle tried to cross, they risked a long fall and a painful death in the mud and shit below.

"Noshi?" Erik called. The box she lived in was older than either of them. Noshi had ended up here after her mother died giving birth to the baby that would have been Noshi's younger brother or sister.

Neither of them knew who their fathers were. No one ever did. Mothers claimed their offspring because they got extra ration credits for the first ten years of the child's life.

III

Pizak moved outside and inhaled the fresh air through the slits in his neck. His eyes saw easily in the drifting yellow mist. The Diorites were native to this world, and over the last thousand years had imposed their will and technology on a dozen other planets.

You will be late. Tosai, his breed-mate and co-genitor of their offspring, warned with a touch of her feelers down his dorsal line.

Enjoy your day of rest, Tosai. Pizak flowed away from their apartment and joined the other commuters going to their duty shifts.

Administrator Pizak, attend Governor K'zyn with priority.

The presence of Narsk, the primary attendant of the governor, flowed strongly into Pizak's consciousness.

Pizak acknowledged the request of attendant Narsk. Moving into the line that would take him to the governor's tower, Pizak reviewed the likely reasons for the summons.

K'zyn would have received Pizak's latest report on the human population. They continued to reproduce in frustratingly low numbers once the infant mortality rate was taken into account. They were savage, unpredictable, and remarkably adaptable. Pizak found the species fascinating, and that alone put him at odds with every other government official.

Administrator Pizak, to see Governor K'zyn, he announced to the entrance wall. It shimmered in welcome and he glided through the gel, confirming his identity to the myriad security systems as he went.

The lift platform arrived as Pizak approached. He gestured greetings to those he passed. They waved in response. Without a physical connection, it was simply a courtesy.

Pizak's mood remained somber as he ascended to the governor's office.

K'zyn occupied a space larger than the apartment Pizak currently shared with Tosai. The mottled pigments of K'zyn's skin were faded, a sign of his advanced years. He answered to no one but the Diorite Congress, and he controlled what they were told.

I acknowledge you, Governor K'zyn. Pizak expressed his greeting in a mental projection of swirling colors.

Pizak, welcome. Juice?

My gratitude, Pizak replied.

K'zyn indicated that Pizak should help himself. He took a cup, curling a tentacle around it and staring into the green contents.

I have read your recent report, the governor announced. The patterns of his communication swirled around Pizak. *Your observations are insightful and detailed as usual.*

My gratitude. Pizak sipped his juice.

It does highlight some areas of concern, K'zyn continued. The projection altered to shades indicating concern and the support of a mentor to a favored student.

The enclosure sanitation? I have requested upgrades to the systems. But-

Sanitation is not our concern, K'zyn interrupted.

I await your wisdom, Pizak expressed formally.

The military faculty require more humans for the training program. Your report indicates a continuing decline in physical state among them. If we cannot provide suitable candidates, the program will be terminated.

I understand, Governor. I can recommend a range of solutions to this trend. All, however, will come at a cost.

Indeed. K'zyn's tentacles drooped in a way which showed his sorrow at this fact. *Secure a contingent. Minimum of twelve specimens with physical attributes above seventy-five rating.*

Twelve...? A tremor rolled through Pizak's feelers. *Governor, the maturity of specimens takes time. We cannot guarantee twelve over seventy-five.*

It will reflect badly if they are not procured by shift's end.

Pizak felt the juice souring in his digestive tract. K'zyn would never be blamed for poor quality recruits into the military faculty's training program. That narrow focus would fall on Administrator Pizak, keeper of the dome and its primitive occupants.

By your grace, Pizak said, again addressing the governor formally. K'zyn indicated that the administrator was dismissed.

Pizak left the office, gliding over the smooth floor to his own work area. Here, behind a wall of screens, he could observe the humans who lived in the atmosphere of nitrogen and toxic oxygen under the glass of the dome.

IV

"Noshi," Erik called. A scrap of cloth that worked as a door flickered. Erik took that as a sign his friend was home. He finished the perilous crossing and tapped on the wall. "I've got some bread. A fresh disc, from Mek's stall."

The cloth door jerked back, and Noshi stared at Erik with large, milky eyes. She had always been blind, but could find her way around the dome better than anyone who could see.

"You'd better hide then," she said.

Erik slipped inside and the curtain fell back into place at his back.

"I can smell it," Noshi said. The ceiling of the room was too low for them to stand fully upright. Noshi sat cross-legged on the floor and patted the boards in front of her. Erik sat down, wriggling his shirt up to extract the disc of bread.

"Shit," he said.

"What is wrong?" Noshi's nostrils flared.

"It's broken," Erik said, his hands filled with the crumbled remains of the dry loaf.

Noshi leaned forward, long hair falling over her face. Erik reminded himself not to look down the loose neck of her ragged dress.

"Give me some," Noshi insisted.

Erik filled her hands with the crumbs. He scooped up more of it from the stained folds of his pants and brushed himself down, salvaging enough for a second handful.

Noshi lifted her hands to her face and inhaled. "It is fresh, but he has put less flour in it than usual." She squeezed her hands into fists, compressing the powdery bread into a solid lump. She nibbled at it while Erik did the same with his portion.

"You in good trouble this time?" Noshi asked.

"Good enough," Erik agreed.

"Nice knowing you."

"They haven't caught me yet," Erik said through a mouthful of half-chewed bread.

"They will find you. Everyone knows you hang up here."

"I'll fight them."

"The slugs will come and drag you out of the dome and let you choke."

"I'll fight them too." Erik swallowed a lump of bread. Noshi always spoke honestly. It was one of the reasons he liked her so much.

The girl tilted her head, a sure sign she was listening to something Erik couldn't hear. "Calzon's coming for you. Three of them coming up the scaff."

Erik swallowed his mouthful. Pressing the remaining bread into a lump, he handed it to the slight figure who remained cross-legged on the floor.

"If you live long enough, can you fill my can?" Noshi asked. Erik nodded and picked up the plastic water container. Moving to the blanket door, he crouched, ready to strike when the opportunity presented itself.

Outside on the scaffolding, three men climbed with the ease of spiders. They kicked people aside and snarled warnings at those who rose to oppose them. At the final walkway, they paused.

"Erik!" the lead man called out. "We know you're in there."

"Bucket, quit the noise," Noshi scolded from inside.

Bucket flinched. The pale girl was as thin as silk, strong as spider thread, and everyone knew she was a witch.

"We got no scrap with you, Noshi," Bucket said.

"Well, come in then."

Bucket gestured at the man on his left, "Hek, go."

Hek tested the strength of the plank bridge. It creaked under his weight and he crossed it in three quick steps.

At the other side, he turned and grinned at the two behind him, victory giving him courage.

Erik burst out of Noshi's tiny house and tackled Hek around the knees. They both crashed over the edge and dropped out of sight.

"Fuck," Bucket swore. "Bly, get after that little shit."

Bly leapt to obey, dropping from the walkway to a ledge below. Bucket leaned over and took a look. Far below, in the warm mist, he could see Hek's body; broken and still, impaled on a jagged spar. Erik had vanished.

When Calzon finished taking his anger out on Erik, Bucket would make sure whatever was left screamed for a long time.

Turning back, he ducked inside the shelter. Noshi stood up, barely stooping under the low ceiling.

"You come with me," Bucket ordered.

"Where would we go?" Noshi replied.

"Calzon's."

"I thought he preferred boys."

Bucket shrugged. "What's the difference?"

"I'll not climb with you."

Bucket stepped forward and snatched at the girl. She moved with impossible speed. In one moment, she was under his hand; the next, she was letting the blanket door drop in her wake.

"Shit." Bucket ran for the door, cracking his head on the low ceiling as he went. Dazed, he flicked the blanket aside and looked around.

Noshi climbed the scaffolding, heading for the highest limits of the interior wall. Her thin limbs carried her with ease over the flimsy framework. Bucket scowled. Going after her meant getting up amongst the spiders. He hated spiders, the six-legged hexapods as big as a man's head. The farmers liked them because they came down on threads to hunt the rats among the crops at night.

"Fuck it." Bucket started climbing down. He would have enough to explain to Calzon without chasing the girl up the damned wall.

V

Breathing hurt but not enough to stop Erik running. If Hek had died in the fall, then Erik was dead too. The Mess was more than home; it was the entire world. With nowhere else to go, it would be a simple matter of time.

Calzon would have no choice. Killing without authorization would get Erik choked—tossed out to breathe his last moments in the raw atmosphere of the world.

Avoiding the crowded walkways, Erik stayed out of sight as he crept through the cluttered housing units. His first priority was to find a weapon. The best place to do that was the entrance, where the bosses went to meet with the slugs and do their trading.

Erik climbed again. Running with light steps across the uneven roofs of a dozen small houses, he avoided the watchful eyes of Calzon's men below.

An archway marked the airlock where supplies came in and those selected for service went out. Erik lay down and wriggled forward the last few feet to the edge. A ragged group of men and women were gathering at the entrance. One of Calzon's men was walking up and down, inspecting the group as if they were livestock.

The call must have come through, a call for able-bodied men and women to give themselves to service. It was the dream of all young humans to join the mercenary corps and enjoy the glorious life that service promised.

Without further thought, Erik slipped off the roof and dropped to the mud. Keeping his eyes downcast he merged with the group and tried to look older than he was.

"How many?"

Shit—Calzon. Erik froze. Running now would get him beaten and raped. He would end up in the cage until the slugs gave instructions for him to be sent out to choke.

"Twelve," Calzon's lieutenant replied.

"Only twelve?"

"Yeah, volunteers are thin on the ground this month."

Legend had it that Calzon had been a merc, a veteran of service to the Diorite military. Now he ruled over the squats in The Mess. "All right, you mud eaters. You're going to get scanned. If you're sick, or weak, you won't get chose. If you're strong and got fight in ya, then glory be yours."

The volunteers shifted, nervous and excited to be given the chance for something more than living in the stink under the dome.

"Send 'em through." Calzon dismissed the group with a wave before turning on his heel and walking away through the mud.

"Line up, one at a time," the lieutenant ordered. Erik peeked up from under his fringe. The wall inside the arch shimmered and went like clean water.

The first of the volunteers was pushed forward. He hesitated a moment, and then, with a second shove, he took a deep breath and disappeared through the wall of glistening gel.

"Next."

One by one they entered the pulsing wall. It reminded Erik of snot, but somehow clean.

When the woman in front of Erik passed through, the lieutenant's eye fell on Erik. "Hey!" he shouted. "Erik, you little shit, Calzon's going to fuck the life out of you!"

Erik ducked under the lieutenant's swing and dived for the wall. For one long second a hand tore at his shirt as he felt the sickeningly warm press of the gel engulfing him. A moment later, he fell to the floor on the other side.

CHAPTER 2

I

Erik's breath misted and he felt his skin prickling against the cold. A steady breeze washed over him as he lay on a steel grate floor. It took him a moment to register what seemed so strange: the air he was breathing didn't smell of anything.

Shivering, he stood and folded his arms across his chest. The thin material of his shirt did nothing to protect him from the unaccustomed cold.

The strange wall behind him had solidified to the dull grey it had always been. Ahead, metal struck metal with a ringing clang behind a circular metal door. Erik tensed, ready to run and hide or fight if he had to. The door spun open, its iris opening like a flower.

Erik crept closer, steam gushed from hidden vents, bathing him in warm, moist air. Taking another step, he crossed the threshold and the door wound smoothly closed at his back.

The temperature went up and the air filled with a thick steam. Hidden in the mist, angled jets of hot water blasted Erik from all directions, knocking him off his feet and forcing him to hold his breath or risk drowning.

"REMOVE ALL ITEMS OF CLOTHING," an unseen voice boomed. Erik complied, dropping his shoes, pants and shirt on the floor. He heard the water jets activating again and braced himself for the deluge. After a second brutal shower, he sniffed the strange chemical smell that lingered on his skin and hair.

The mist evacuated in a howl of suction fans, revealing a second iris door on the other side of the room. Erik advanced, having no other choice. Full bodysuits with separate boots and gloves hung on racks in the next room. The last of the others who had passed through the wall before Erik were here, dressing and stamping their feet in the strange softness of the fitted boots.

Still waiting to be dragged away and thrown into the open atmosphere, Erik snatched a suit from the rack and pulled it on. The material contracted, pressing comfortably against his skin as it adjusted to his size. The boots and gloves gripped him in the same way.

The other volunteers were in good spirits, grinning and admiring their new wardrobe. If this was a sign of the comforts they could expect in their new lives. They were looking forward to it.

"ONE AT A TIME. STEP FORWARD. STAND IN THE LIGHT," the unseen voice boomed.

A circle of blue light came from the ceiling. The human nearest the light looked around at the others, who watched him closely. With a shrug, he stepped into the vertical beam and waited.

After a moment, the light clicked off. "EXIT THE CHAMBER."

Another round door twirled open, the man walked through, and it closed.

"ONE AT A TIME. STEP FORWARD. STAND IN THE LIGHT."

The cycle repeated itself; each of the freshly washed and dressed volunteers stood in the light and then walked through the door when commanded.

Within two minutes, Erik was one of three humans left in the chamber. A woman took her turn in the light and then stepped through the portal.

The last man had been wheezing since Erik came in from the wash chamber. His chest rose and fell with the effort of breathing, and Erik wondered if he had inhaled water.

The man took his place in the light and after a moment the floor opened under his feet and he dropped. Erik sprang forward, reaching out a hand to grab the man's flailing arm.

"He-help me!" the man gasped, his arms holding him on the rim of the circular hole.

"Grab my hand!" Erik seized him by the wrist and strained

to lift. The air filled with a high-pitched buzzing sound and then a smell of burning flesh.

The man in the hole screamed and Erik fell backward as the opening sealed shut. The man vanished, only his arm remaining, still in Erik's grip.

With a startled cry, Erik tossed the limb away. The shoulder was seared to ashes and much of the skin had burned black.

The smell of charred meat faded with the roar of extraction fans. Erik ran for the door behind him. It remained sealed and he pounded on it, screaming for help.

"STEP FORWARD. STAND IN THE LIGHT." The voice boomed. Erik slid down to the floor, his back pressed against the wall.

"CHAMBER ATMOSPHERE EVACUATING." The voice announced. Erik felt his ears pop and a moment later it became hard to breathe. Crawling he headed for the glowing circle. Spots danced in front of his eyes and a band of steel tightened around his chest. The room swirled with grey mist and Erik collapsed.

II

Pizak reviewed the data streaming in from the physiology scans. The human volunteers barely met the minimum criteria. They would need conditioning beyond the usual training and augmentation. That of course, came at a cost. Pizak knew without referring to the financial files that the program's budget was fully accounted for. Cuts would have to be made somewhere and K'zyn would expect targets to be met regardless.

An alarm sounded. Pizak cancelled it immediately, tuning his sensors to assure himself that no one else in the office area had detected the alert. A human had failed the initial bio-scans and had been terminated. One subject remained and the drop of atmospheric pressure in the assessment chamber had rendered it unconscious.

"Complete bio-metric scan of remaining subject," Pizak ordered. The computer acknowledged the command and the data filled up his screen.

Pizak's tendrils lifted as his interest grew. There was promise in these readings—a genuine candidate for the program.

"Recover human candidate," Pizak ordered. His future and the human's were suddenly aligned. The philosophers would describe this as an omen of note.

III

The smells and sounds Erik awoke to were unfamiliar. A grunting, a sound of arousal though not quite sexual. A scent of cooked meat, spiced and rich. The yeasty odor of bread, baked fresh, still hot from the oven. He struggled to his feet, the instinctive urge to get his share of the food driving him before he was fully aware.

"Hey, Scrap. You hungry?" One of the volunteers, his voice thick with meat juice. It glistened on his lips and dripped off his chin.

Erik slid into a plastic seat, formed to hold the human shape. He snatched a thick slab of the brown flesh from a platter and stuffed it into his mouth before anyone could tell him no.

As he chewed, Erik looked around the table. Everyone was eating, gorging themselves with a plenty that none of them had ever known. He took a fistful of bread, soft and white as Noshi's hair.

After a few mouthfuls, Erik's stomach rebelled. He winced in sudden pain, fearful that it was a trap and he had been poisoned. The man next to him tilted his chin up and let out a rolling belch.

Others laughed, answering with their own vibrant calls. Erik straightened his back and let the rising pressure in his taut belly escape. Someone clapped him on the back and laughed. Erik blinked. It was the first time in memory anyone had struck him without malice.

They feasted until the platters were wiped clean and the

absorbent material of the table was pooled with congealing grease. The men and women groaned in satisfaction, pulling away from the table and wiping their faces with the sleeves of the bodysuits they wore.

"If this is what we can look forward to working for the slugs, then all-fucking-right!" someone called to the room. They responded with cheers.

Erik kept watching the reflective walls, wondering who was watching them, how they were being assessed, and what was expected of them in return for the gifts given.

Aside from the table, the room held simple beds, stacked two high. One above and one below, softer than anything that Erik had ever slept on. It was to the bunks that the volunteers now turned, stretching out and sighing with contentment. They didn't fight over who got what bed, instead giving way to each other and settling without incident.

Erik returned to the bunk where he had awoken. Lying down in the creases of his own outline, he tried to make sense of the experience.

Around him, the room settled into sleep. Erik kept himself awake as long as possible, waiting to see what would happen when everyone was unconscious. Soon even his eyes slipped shut and he slept again.

IV

Noshi sat up, the intensity of her dream startling her to wakefulness. As was her custom, she took two deep breaths, in through the nose and out through the mouth. She settled in a cross-legged position, focusing on the dream and reviewing it before it slipped from her consciousness.

Smells, textures, and sounds formed a three-dimensional world around her. She knew everyone in The Mess by their smell, the sound of the footsteps, and even the way they breathed. In her dream, she detected familiar figures, including

Erik, and it gave her hope that he might still be alive.

The voice that spoke to Noshi did not come from the dream. It stood outside it, observing like she did. "Among the Diorites, *Ka'tharis*, omen in standard language of humans, have an influence in all aspects of personal and professional life."

"*Ka'tharis*," Noshi whispered.

"The source of all omens is not in the metaphysical or spiritual constructs. For Diorites have no concept of such things. They observe and calculate, recognizing that randomness, chaos, and coincidence are unopposable forces in the great machine of the Universe."

"I don't understand," Noshi whispered. Focusing her mind, she pushed deeper into the fading memory of the dream, seeking the light caress of the whispers that brushed against her like floating strands of web.

Pizak floated in the warm sub-consciousness of *metra*. The natural process of physical renewal through meditation was a daily ritual that focused the mind and sharpened the mental acuity. Like every other minute of his daily shift, the time for meditation was allocated, monitored, and assessed.

During intimate moments with Tosai, when they connected for pleasure and not for the purpose of producing offspring, they would both enter this state. Laying themselves bare, their innermost psyche revealed. Entrusting another with your most vulnerable thoughts and being gifted the same in return was the definition of love.

The sensation of an unknown presence pressing in Pizak's mind startled him.

I don't understand, the stranger's voice whispered.

I am alone, Pizak expressed indignantly. Among a species who communicated across a range of energy spectrums, solitude was an unassailable right.

Ka'tharis, the alien presence insisted. *Can omens be denied?*

For Pizak, reviewing ancient philosophy guided his metra. In this deeply relaxed state, he could sharpen his mind like a blade on a whetstone through analysis of the ancient theorems.

Who are you? Pizak asked. The sense drifting around him had no familiar aspect.

Noshi, the presence replied. It's communication took the unusual form of sound. *Are you in my dream?*

Pizak pondered the meaning of the word. A dream, a metra-like process, but unguided. A human brain activity.

You are human? Pizak's consciousness rippled. A human connecting in metra?

Or am I in your dream? Noshi continued.

I do not dream.

Then what is this?

Pizak gave the question some thought. *You are Noshi, human female?*

Yes?

Have you exchanged consciousness with others?

I... don't think so?

Her tone told Pizak that she had not. This was a *Ka'tharis* of the first order. One arising without forecast or prediction.

Remain where you are. Communicate with no one, Pizak instructed.

Am I to be punished? Noshi asked.

I will do what I can to ensure that you are not.

With a shift of his will and a change in his bio-chemistry, Pizak ejected himself from the meditative state.

At his work terminal, he issued instructions to the human agents inside the dome.

CHAPTER 3

I

Calzon dressed without paying attention. His clothes were little better than the rags worn by most of the inhabitants of The Mess. He liked his boots though—pliable leather, worn soft, with wrap-around straps that kept them firm on his feet and calves.

Shala lay in a pile of his blankets, still, warm, and soft. He didn't want to leave her, but the message had been clear. Bring Noshi to the gate.

This had something to do with that little shit, Erik. Jimin had reported that the kid had slipped into the airlock with the other volunteers. The Diorites would either toss him out into the atmosphere or send him back. If he came back in here, Calzon would make him wish he had choked in the yellow sulfur mists outside the dome.

Calzon's men fell into step behind him as he stepped down into the mud and marched off towards the wall.

"What's the plan, boss?" Jimin asked. He would do anything to win back Calzon's favor. Calzon intended to keep that loaded weapon holstered for as long as possible.

"Find the blind kid, Noshi."

"We crossed her off before," Jimin said.

"Yeah, we're gonna cross her off again."

"Bad luck to kill a witch," someone else muttered. Calzon turned in mid-stride. He pushed Jimin aside and slammed a fist into the second man's face, sending him sprawling in the mud.

"If there's any of you shit smears that are afraid of a blind kid, then get the fuck out of my line of sight." He glared at each of them until they dropped their gaze. Jimin's eyes never left the ground.

Calzon led his crew up the rickety scaffolding and walkways

of the wall. The shelters up here were a maze of hovels and lean-tos. The entire structure creaked and whispered with each step. The boss kept his face expressionless and climbed. He hated heights, not that he would ever admit that to anyone. Weakness, Calzon's mother had always said, would get you killed.

"Which of these shit holes is hers?" Calzon asked. Jimin pointed at a flapping blanket door.

"Noshi?" Calzon called from the other side of the plank bridge. "You need to come out here. I need to talk to you."

"Calzon." Noshi's reply was not a question. She knew who he was and the men behind him shuffled nervously.

The blanket was pulled aside and the white-haired girl slipped out to stand in the twilight gloom. "You are to take me to the main gate," Noshi advised.

"Is that right?" Calzon had the same instructions, but he would be damned if a scrap of a kid was going to tell him what to do.

"Yes," Noshi replied.

Her calm confidence unnerved Calzon. He would make her afraid of him. She needed to be afraid of him. That was the source of his power.

"Get your ass down to mud," he growled.

Noshi pulled a ragged shawl tighter around her shoulders and stepped lightly across the bridge. "You brought Jimin, Kalus, Morgy, and Depa?" Noshi turned her clouded eyes on each of them as she spoke their names. "I am flattered."

Calzon raised a hand and waved it in front of the girl's eyes. She didn't blink or react. "Blind as a cabbage," he said.

"I have always been blind, Calzon. Yet I see far more than you."

"You talk a lot of shit," Calzon sneered with a confidence that could not hide his unease.

"The Diorites are waiting," Noshi reminded him.

"The what now?" Jimin asked.

"Slugs, spider brain. She's talking about the slugs." Calzon pounced on easier prey. "Hey!" Noshi had slipped past them and was climbing down the scaffolding to the walkway with a casual poise.

"Move, you fucks," Calzon snarled and followed her.

II

Noshi sensed the people around her. Their breath, the rustle of their clothes. The spectrum of scents that clung to everybody. It created a unique perception more detailed than sight.

People moved out of her way, and she walked directly to the airlock gate. The scents here mingled with the low-frequency thrum of the Diorite machinery. She waited for Calzon and his gang to catch up.

The men at the airlock were gone, returned to their hovels until needed again. Noshi inhaled the cold steel smell of the heavy door. She had no idea what lay beyond. If anyone did, they never spoke of it.

At a control panel, Calzon keyed in a code, secret to anyone who didn't rely on their ears as their primary sense. Noshi re-played the beeping sound in her head—seven buttons, seven tones. The door slid open, revealing the glistening wall of pulsing gel. Noshi hesitated. The smell was new to her and for the first time in her life, she felt unsure of her next step.

"Go through," Calzon said behind her. "That's the orders."

Noshi extended a hand until her fingers passed into the gel, which pressed against her touch like warm flesh.

"Ain't got all cycle," Calzon growled and shoved Noshi forward. She stumbled and passed through the barrier. The airlock hissed shut behind her.

Noshi coughed, spitting the mouthful of gel that threatened to choke her. The surface under her feet was metal, a lattice grille of intersecting panels. The air was warm, wet, and odorless. It flowed like breath over Noshi and she waited, taking everything in, orienting herself in this new, strange space.

Noshi. The voice from her dream echoed around her.

"I am here," she replied, her voice bouncing off the steel walls.

Pizak continued, *The section you are in is an extension of the containment unit. The atmosphere is controlled and suitable for your biochemistry.*

Noshi did not understand most of his words, but the Diorite's voice in her head sounded friendly. "What do you want me for?"

For the future, Pizak replied.

"I don't understand," Noshi said after a moment of silence.

You are not required to understand. You should only accept that I have a requirement and you are the first human recorded who meets certain specifications.

His words remained meaningless to Noshi; she understood that he had something for her to do. She could wait to see what that was.

Move forward, Pizak commanded. Noshi did not move for a count of three. Then she took a step.

Her feet described the pattern of the floor and she followed it to the other side of the chamber. Another door slid open and she passed through.

Pizak's voice rolled through her. *Remove your clothing. You will be cleaned and new attire provided.*

Water flowed from a spout. Noshi moved toward it and felt the air temperature rising. She removed the ragged cloth of her dress and let the shower pour over her, filling her senses.

Something in the water lifted the dirt from her skin and she felt clean for the first time in her life.

The clothes provided felt softer than any fabric she had known before. They had a soft scent she could not place. She dressed, working out how it fitted by the shape and sleeves.

There is no one I can assign to assist you, Pizak said.

"I never had any help before," Noshi reminded him. She knew nothing about Diorites except the sound of their voices through the broadcasts. The other humans called them slugs, and Noshi had always wondered if slugs were beautiful.

"Is this right?" Noshi stood, arms at her sides, ready for inspection.

You are correctly attired, Pizak said. *Move forward, through the door.*

Noshi found herself in what felt like a larger space. The slight sounds did not return to her as quickly in here.

Associate yourself with your surroundings. You will be housed in this space.

"For how long?" Noshi spoke to the darkness and it remained silent.

She explored the room—soft furnishings, a chair, a bed. Things she had only heard of from other's descriptions. Food smells around a slot in the wall. Her fingers brushed over a panel of recessed buttons. The gentle pressure made something beep. "Select food option," a voice said.

"I can't see," Noshi whispered.

The voice recited a menu of unknown items. Noshi made a couple of selections. The panel opened, and a tray slid out. Noshi took it to a table and found a seat. Exploring the tray, she found soft mush, something that had the texture of bread, and other objects she couldn't recognize.

It was the best food she had ever tasted.

III

For Noshi, the transition from sleep to wakefulness meant a return of sensation. It always took her a moment to confirm she was no longer dreaming.

Noshi. Pizak's presence spoke to her in a way she felt more than heard.

"Yes?" She sat up, ears straining to detect any sound out of place.

Adorn yourself. Then eat. Today we begin.

Breakfast had different textures and flavors than her previous meal. Noshi ate more than she had in her life. If this all ended today, she would treasure the memories.

Pizak's presence washed over her. *Follow this sound.* A tone called to her. Noshi stood up and moved in that direction.

Access the cabinet, Pizak instructed. Noshi extended her arms, feeling nothing but space for several steps. Then her hands found a shape in the wall. It slid open under her touch.

Adorn yourself. The garment will provide you with atmosphere.

The clothes inside were different to the one-piece bodysuit Noshi currently wore. She found boots attached to the ends of the trousers, gloves at the ends of the arms, and a close-fitting helmet with a bulbous, blank face.

Noshi struggled into the unfamiliar suit. It was thicker and fit easily over the clothes she currently wore. The helmet clicked into place, making Noshi take a deep breath in near panic. Then air flowed over her face and she breathed easily. "I can't feel anything." For the first time in her life, she felt truly blind.

Activating sensors.

Sensation rippled through Noshi's fingers and feet. She felt the floor as if she were barefoot, and the textured surface of the enclosed suit as if the gloves were gone.

Can you feel my presence, Pizak asked, his enunciation strange, the question phrased as flatly as a statement.

"Yes." Noshi almost laughed with relief. She could hear everything. The gentle hum of the machinery in the walls. The slight movement of her body and the quiet passage of her breath.

Bring yourself to my current location, Pizak instructed.

"Where are you?" Noshi replied.

Find me. It is the first lesson.

"I don't understand." Noshi hated the weakness of her words. She stood in silence, a growing sense of frustration and embarrassment filling her until she thought the suit might explode.

"Think," she scolded herself. "You are wearing some strange machine. It gives you air. Protection like the dome. Pizak wants you to go out into his world. Into the open air. Where you will die."

Life in the dome had been a constant struggle for survival for everyone. Noshi's reputation had kept the worst assaults at bay. She lived with the constant fear that at any moment, someone might see through her mystery and she would become a slave to someone stronger. Someone like Pizak.

Noshi moved around the room, marking off the food dispenser, the cabinet where the suit had come from, and the door that led back towards the dome. On the opposite side of the room she found a second door. This one had a panel on it that did not respond to her touch.

She explored the door and found a circular disc with rods radiating from it. Noshi moved her hands and gripped the rods, she twisted the wheel until it loosened and then spun easily.

The door slid open and Noshi moved into a new space, close and confined. A small, box-like room. Reaching out she felt the walls and with a stretch, her gloved fingers brushed the ceiling.

The door closed behind her, startling Noshi into a moment of panic. She fumbled at the door. Finding the same spoked wheel on the inside, Noshi tugged on it with no effect.

A shushing sound swirled around her. The suit pressed tight and then expanded as the internal atmosphere adjusted to the change in pressure. With tentative steps, Noshi walked out of the tiny chamber and into infinity.

IV

The limits of Noshi's universe had always been defined by the dome; it gave scope to everything. Now she sensed no walls, no curving dome that shaped the acoustics of her surroundings. Instead, there was only absence. A strange emptiness that filled her with vertigo. Sinking into a crouch, Noshi pressed her hands against the ground, a hard surface with lines in regular patterns. In a crouch, she walked on hands and feet, tracing the lines, learning the pattern and regaining her composure. Standing tall, she took a step, relying on her feet to guide her, to follow the pattern.

Her hand found a rail a moment before her feet; turning, she walked its path. Her left-hand skimmed over the surface, the certainty of it reassuring in this strange world. Noshi had wondered how she would know she had found Pizak, or if she was going in the right direction. Let him make contact if she strayed from the correct path.

Something curled around her extended hand. Something more pliable than fingers, like the tip of a rope. Noshi froze at the strange touch. "Pizak?"

Know me as Mukari. The voice in her head sounded similar to Pizak's but different.

"Noshi."

Pizak has ordered you.

To Noshi, it should have been a question, but like Pizak's voice in her mind, it lacked the essentials of tone.

"Pizak invited me to find him."

Invited…

"Asked me to find him."

Explanation for action. Again, a question delivered as a statement.

"Pizak spoke of, uh, Kartharis."

Ka'tharis. You will need to be prepared. Ka'tharis indicates uncertain probabilities.

"I don't understand."

Ka'tharis does not require comprehension. Perception comes with memory.

"Can you tell me where Pizak is? I don't want to keep him waiting."

Your sensory organs are inefficient. You have congenital defects.

Noshi didn't bother asking what that meant. "I need to find Pizak."

Affirmative.

"Pizak," Noshi stated.

Continue on your present path. Enter structure. Ascend to the fourth level. Pizak is located.

"Thank you."

Gratitude acknowledged.

The tentacle withdrew and Noshi continued her journey. The rail and the marks in the tiled floor guided her until she walked into a wall. Exploring the flat surface, she found a door, which opened. Reminding herself that she was being tested, Noshi stepped through and felt the door slide shut behind her.

"State required level." This voice lacked the inference and tonality of a living voice.

Noshi wondered who or what spoke. "Ascend to level four," she replied.

The space around her moved. Noshi pressed her hand against the wall, disorientated by the sudden sensation of rising. By the time she remembered to breathe, the motion stopped and the door opened.

"Level four," the flat voice said.

"Thank you," Noshi stepped out. "Pizak," she said.

Noshi. Welcome. A warm familiarity engulfed her.

"Why am I here? What do you want from me?"

You are unique among your species.

"Aren't we each unique?" Noshi had been told that there were no other humans left except those in the dome. Their species was nearly extinct, one of millions of life forms in the Galaxy that had flared brightly, spread like an outbreak of disease and then had been crushed by a stronger force, their own greed, or a stop in reproduction.

By what qualification are you all unique.

"We are few."

Your species utilizes only five senses. You detect light on a short spectrum. You detect vibrations in atmosphere. You have sensory nerve cells across the surface of your bodies. You taste with the same orifice you use to communicate and you detect molecules with a limited sensitivity through your respiratory system.

"I can't see," Noshi reminded him.

Yes. In this you are unique. You are the only human born with a sensory deficit of this degree who has survived beyond infancy.

"They died as… babies?"

Yes.

"How?"

Your statement has no identifiable purpose.

Noshi tried again. "How did they die?"

We do not record the specifics of the instances. Just the numbers.

"How many?" Noshi asked.

Eighty-seven. Since the establishment of the reservation.

"Is that a lot?"

It is not a significant number, Pizak replied.

"But… one survivor is?" Noshi breathed through the silence that followed. The audio system built into the suit told her ears that Pizak was still nearby. Even inside the suit, with its own air supply, she could smell something different through the filters. A specific scent that she associated with the strange presence of Pizak.

Move forward until advised to cease, Pizak said.

Noshi did so.

Extend your right hand. The furniture you feel has been crafted to fit your body form. Recline in a manner comfortable for you.

Noshi slid into the seat. Softer than anything she had ever felt, it molded around her, and she had a strange flash of memory from the womb.

We will now begin, Pizak said. Rope like tendrils touched her helmet and then, to her shock, she felt them caress her face, exploring her features with light brush strokes similar to how she discovered details in anything new. It felt oddly familiar to be on the receiving end of such an inspection.

The tendrils spread over her forehead and temples. To Noshi it felt like a fist opening, spreading fingers pressing against her skin. The contact pulsed and her world filled with light.

CHAPTER 4

I

During the first month, every daylight cycle began with the braying of an electronic alarm. Erik and the other volunteers from the dome had less than a minute to roll out of their cots, straighten and stow the beds, pull on their one-piece bodysuits and boots, and be standing ramrod straight in precisely marked positions.

At fifty-five seconds, the door at the end of the barracks room opened and Kill-Sergeant Crysto marched in screaming about how useless they all were.

Like everyone else in the barracks, Erik hated Crysto. She was one of five kill-sergeants who screamed at the squad from the first alarm until they passed out on their cots at the end of the day.

Crysto kicked the cot panel behind the recruit stationed next to Erik. The bed unfolded from the wall and the kill-sergeant tore the bedding off the foam base and sent it flying across the room. "What the fuck is this shit?!" Crysto screamed. You think this is stowed? You shit-eating fuck."

"No, Kill-Sergeant!" the young recruit bellowed.

"Stow this shit! Stow it like you mean it! The rest of you dumb-fucks! Get the fuck out of here!"

The squad stampeded for the door, bursting out of the barracks shed and forming up on the dusty ground outside.

Kill-Sergeant Mosan barked at them while they fell into line, yelling until they were straight and standing to his liking.

"Today you learn to live in your own portable atmosphere!" The armored suit stood on a metal frame. It was fitted to a human shape with dark armored plates on the torso, arms, and legs. "The self-contained atmosphere apparatus will be your entire world.

You will live and die inside this suit. You will traverse the yellow deserts, the green mountains, and the forests and plains of this world and a hundred others with your pasty asses packed inside one of these suits!"

Mosan pulled an armored helmet off the back of the rack. It had a clear face plate of curved plastic and a dark, close fitting helm that connected to the suit's collar. "This is your new face! After today this is the only head I ever want to see. It will be your fucking window on the world. Through this you will see your enemy. You will kill your enemy and you will emerge victorious on the field of battle."

The kill-sergeant's demonstrated how to don the suits and yelled at the squad while they struggled to get the unfamiliar armor on and locked in position. On Erik's slight frame the armor weighed a ton. He felt a rising sense of panic as the suit contracted to fit him. He would never be able to move in this fucking thing.

When the helmet was locked in place he took a panicked breath and felt air waft over his face.

"Right now, you cannot move!" Kill-Sergeant Mosan's voice roared in the squad's helmets. "You will stand until you understand!"

Following the yelled instructions, Erik and his squad went through a series of operational exercises. They drilled until the communications system, the life-support controls, and the Heads-Up Display that streamed essential information across the inside of their face plates were as familiar as their own thoughts.

Once they mastered the internal systems, the hydraulics controls were unlocked. The powered armor lightened and even Erik could walk with ease. With the kill-sergeants screaming at them, the squad ran up and down the grounds until the suits were covered in dust and the troopers inside were streaming with sweat and gasping for air. They marched and ran up and down for hours until Erik was on the verge of collapse. The kill-kergeants moved the squad on to the same obstacle course they had conquered every day since their training started.

The suits didn't make it easier. The walls were still high, the mud still thick. With the added mass of the suit, more than one trooper got fouled crawling under wire.

"Stand up! Stand up, you fucks!"

Erik swayed on his feet. The moisture streaming down his face was absorbed by the suit lining and, from the taste of it, recycled into his fresh water supply.

"Get in fucking line!" The squad shuffled into position and locked their legs to keep them standing.

"You will stand there until you are ordered to move!"

"Yes, Kill-Sergeant!"

The sergeants walked away and the squad remained standing. Erik stared at the helmet in front of him, waiting for something to happen. The chronometer on his HUD vanished.

"The fuck…?" he muttered. "Hey, my chrono went out."

"Mine too." The response echoed through the squad.

"Kill-Sergeant? I think there's a malfu-" Erik's comms system clicked off and the clear screen went dark.

"Stand steady!" The kill-sergeant's voice roared in his comms.

A sense of vertigo washed over Erik. With no vision to balance with and a blacked-out HUD, he was entirely cut off. He wondered how the others in the squad were doing. Were they also isolated or were they all standing around laughing their asses off at him swaying and trying to stay on his feet?

Time meant nothing in the sensory deprivation of the locked-down suit. The only way Erik could tell he was still alive was by counting the slow respiration of each breath. In… out. Still… alive…

By the time his breathing had slowed and panic had given way to boredom, Erik was sure they had been forgotten. Maybe he was trapped in this suit now? What happened when the air ran out?

Erik started to hyperventilate, his breath becoming ragged as panic flooded him again. He tried to move, to flex any part of the suit and break free. It remained immobile and added to his frantic unease. There was no escape. He was going to die in this tiny prison.

The screaming sounded far away. Erik couldn't be sure it was him. His ears were ringing and the air had run out. Now he was going to die.

Muffled sounds came through the suit. Something struck Erik hard enough to rock him on his feet. He struggled to retain his balance until a second strike pushed him over.

Lying in the dirt, Erik waited for his humiliation to end. No one activated his helmet so he lay there in the dark, tears mixing with the sweat dripping off his face.

II

You are speaking, Pizak's presence was suffocating.

I'm sorry, Noshi clenched her eyes shut and took a deep breath.

Again.

She opened her mind to the flowing current of mental activity that swirled around her. Seeing it was the first lesson, becoming one with it, was the next step.

The mental exercises Pizak had her repeating endlessly could not detract from the wonder she felt at the experience of sight.

Pizak had explained that her eyes were deformed; the optic nerves were undeveloped and she would never see. Her abilities allowed her to bypass the physical organs of her senses and to comprehend a world she had no concept of.

To Noshi, light was both terrifying and fascinating.

She understood light was the reflection of photons on a spectrum. She also saw electro-magnetic frequencies, which she learned were more than colors—this was energy. Energy gave everything form and purpose. The cilia that covered a Diorite's head were sensitive receptors for frequencies across the energy spectrum. Through the waving fronds they communicated across vast distances and directed their conquest of entire worlds.

"Conquer... it means to destroy?" Noshi had asked.

It means to adapt, Pizak replied. *The Diorite Commonwealth brings our technology to new worlds. We bring peace to troubled civilizations. We bring a future to worlds without hope.*

"Like the old Earth?" Through Pizak and the growing confidence of her strengthening connection with the network of the Diorite Commonwealth, Noshi learned the truth of human history.

Her people were explorers who left a blue world in another part of the galaxy to set foot on the sister worlds of their own star system. Then, on the wings of emerging technology, they launched themselves across the vast emptiness of the interstellar void. Generations passed and human civilization collapsed.

The Helos were the agents of your species destruction, Pizak told her. This was confirmed by everything Noshi learned during the hours she explored the Diorite archives. The Helos were an enemy without mercy who had destroyed billions of humans. The Diorites had rescued her species from extinction, protecting them and giving them sanctuary in domed reservations on a handful of worlds.

The message from the Diorites was always clear: *Without us, your species would be extinct.*

III

"This weapon is your life! Without it, you are nothing. With this weapon, you will defeat any enemy. Never let it out of your sight. Never put it down. You will sleep with it, eat with it, and shit with it. You will carry it with you to the glory of battle."

The rifle was bulky and without the powered armor to support it, Erik was sure he would barely be able to lift it. In his suit, he could heft it, aim it, and fire it with an accuracy of 94%. Holding the weapon, his rifle, Erik felt strong. Invincible. All he needed now was an enemy that he could kill with it.

CHAPTER 5

I

Erik spat blood into his respirator and blinked the sweat from his eyes.

"Get the fuck out of the mud, you piece of shit." The voice of Kill-Sergeant Mosan, the man Erik hated more than anyone he had ever met, screamed in his ear. It would be easier to sink into the mud and drown. To let the impossible weight of the gear he wore drag him into darkness. To do so would let Mosan win and that would hurt more than standing up.

On leaden legs, Erik stood. He lifted his rifle until it was across his chest and he started running. Each step sinking to the tops of his boots in the muck. The trick was to lift your knees high, clear the mud, and keep moving forward. Mosan moved on to scream at the other troopers who were still crawling.

"Stand up or die!" This was one of several catch phrases Mosan and the other trainers screamed constantly.

Erik stayed on his feet. The end of the section was in sight. He glanced back into the swirling yellow mist, checking on the progress of the rest of Grid Squad Cable while ignoring the burn in his muscles and lungs.

Each day of the ten-cycle exercise, a squad member was promoted to squad leader. This meant more abuse, more work, and a responsibility for the lives of the other recruits. No one volunteered for the role. The kill-sergeants chose someone, seemingly at random. Erik had thirteen hours of squad leadership left. He was counting the minutes until he could pass the burden on to someone else.

The mud gave way to gravel, and the squad jogged up a shifting slope of loose rock that shifted constantly underfoot. Once it got moving, the scree could become a landslide and would bury anyone unlucky enough to fall.

At the top, Erik stopped to catch his breath. Behind him a stream of troopers clawed their way through the mud and up the hill. As they reached the crest, Erik reached out a hand and helped his best friend, Timber, the last few steps. "Good run man."

"Thought you were going to stay in the mud," Timber gasped.

Erik had no breath left for a comeback. He pushed Timber on and helped the next trooper crest the summit. The troopers did not fall. They stayed on their feet, chests heaving, clouds of vapor expelling from their respirators, their masks clear of the condensation which ran down their faces.

In the first days of their training one of the recruits had died after a malfunction in his respirator. The man had panicked. In the throes of his claustrophobia he managed to rip the sealed mask off his face. Exposure to the sulfur dioxide atmosphere had melted his lungs in seconds. He died in agony with bloody foam spilling down his chin. Mosan made everyone take a good long look at what happened if you panicked. It was a lesson they never forgot.

The trainers wore the same respirators and ran the same course. They didn't carry the same amount of war gear as the troopers, but they did spend all day screaming at the trainees.

"Thirty seconds!" Mosan yelled through the comms.

Erik focused on his breathing, flexing his muscles and letting the pain work itself out. Using his tongue, he snagged the nutrient tube inside his mask and took a long swallow of liquid life.

"Ten seconds!" Mosan roared. The squad assumed their ready positions. "Move, you motherfuckers!"

Erik led the way as they charged across the dry plateau at the top of the hill and toward the rock formations that led down to a flowing river of sulfuric acid.

Sharp crystal formations of yellow sulfur and dull green apatite crunched underfoot. Timber ran past Erik, leaping from crystal outcropping to rocky bluff as he took the lead in the race to the river bank.

"Later, bitches!" Timber crowed as he increased his lead.

Erik moved by reflex, seeing the fractures in crystal formations, knowing in mid-stride if the ground would hold him.

Ten feet below, Timber jumped again. The apatite shattered as he landed, throwing him off balance. He recovered quickly, twisting and leaping across the gap to the next formation. He seized a solid chunk of sulfur in one hand and swinging from it until he found a foot hold.

Erik threw himself into space, slamming into the angled edge of the same outcrop. His arms numbed with the shock of impact, he hung there, shoulder to shoulder with Timber.

"You trying to get yourself burned?" he asked over the squad comms channel.

"The burn is how you learn," Timber replied.

"The fuck are you two shit-stains doing?" Mosan cut in over the troopers' laughter.

"Training hard, Kill-Sergeant!" Erik said.

"Fucking circle-jerk. If I get there and you two fucks are sucking face, I will burn you myself."

"Yes, Kill-Sergeant!" both troopers replied with enthusiasm. Pulling themselves up, they continued the descent, arriving at the edge of the river just ahead of the final members of the squad.

"What is your purpose?!" Mosan roared.

"To kill!" the squad screamed in unison.

"How will you achieve that purpose?!"

"Be faster! Be stronger! Be better!"

"The fuck you say?!"

"Faster! Stronger! Better!" The shout in their ear pieces was deafening.

"Gimme a hundred!"

The squad dropped prone and began doing pushups with a metronome synchronicity.

Erik put the burning pain in his muscles out of mind and thought about Noshi. The last time he saw her and the bread they shared.

"One hundred pushups, one hundred and twenty seconds." Mosan barked. "Any less, we will start again. No man left behind. Everyone wins. Everyone suffers."

The troopers rose and fell until Mosan gave the order to get on their feet.

"There's a nice spot to set up some hab-tents and get some sweet shut-eye on the other side of the river. Get there and you get sack time. Now move your asses!"

Their armored suits were protected by high-density plastic plating. The material was acid resistant, bulletproof, and light-weight. The sulfuric acid wouldn't be a problem. The depth and the current would be.

For the first time all day, Mosan and his fell kill-sergeants were silent, giving the squad a chance to solve the problem for themselves. Erik knew it was a test. Everything was a test. You either passed, or you died.

"How deep do you think that shit is?" Timber asked.

"Balls deep," Erik replied, watching the twist and curl of the currents.

Pikila shouldered her rifle. "Fuck it, let's go. Last one over cleans my suit." She started towards the swirling yellow water. The others shrugged and fell into step with her.

"Hold up," Erik said. As squad leader, he was meant to be taking the lead and showing his potential.

"Why? Can't you swim?" Pikila sneered and the others laughed on cue.

"We all cross together—it'll be easier. Like how little spiders cross open space between threads."

"The fuck you talking about, shithead?" Pikila bristled. She had fought almost everyone in the squad, earning their respect by being tougher than them.

"We're a squad, we're meant to work together. You go charging into that on your own, you could end up dead. Then we have to waste time and energy dragging your ass out. Maybe more of us die and we have to pull them out too. I don't want to have to carry more than one of you through the rest of the hike."

Pikila's eyes narrowed behind the transparent panel of her facemask. "Runt like you can barely carry his own shit," she said. "Let alone one of us."

"I know, right? So, we link up. Join arms and lock in. Start up there a way, then walk with the current so we come out the other side right where we want to be." Erik linked arms with Timber and demonstrated how it would work.

Herk laughed. "Ain't you two cute. You gonna dance now, or just fuck?"

Erik ignored him. It was weird how Herk had a real problem with two men touching each other.

"Hold your shit, Herk," Pikila snapped. "You heard our squad leader. Rest of you, cozy up."

The troopers fell into line, forming two lines with their arms interlinked. "Now, like on the p'rade floor. We all step in time," Erik said. "Left, left, left."

The linked chain of troopers moved into the water, each body strengthening their fellows against the onslaught of the current. First in line, Erik reached the middle of the river. The dark fluid swirled around them, now reaching up to his shoulders. The current pushed at him like Mosan standing on his chest.

"Fuck!" Timber yelled as he lost his footing.

"Hold the fucking line!" Erik set his feet. The ground underfoot was softer than he anticipated. The rest of the line stayed upright, bring Timber back on an even keel. Then Erik's next step went into a hole.

Timber yanked Erik up, bringing him above the surface, fluid streaming off his helmet and facemask. "Hole," Erik explained.

"You're just too fucking short, runt." Timber's face showed the strain of holding Erik up.

"What's the fucking holdup!?" Mosan cut in.

"Squad leader Erik, Kill-Sergeant!" Pikila yelled.

"Trooper Erik, you get your short-ass over that river or I will personally strip you!"

"Yes, Kill-Sergeant!" Erik reached out with one foot and probed the mud for purchase. Something curled around his ankle and jerked him off his feet.

"Fuck!" The river went dark as Erik was dragged under. The pressure sensors in his leg armor gave feedback that told him he caught by something tentacle like. It ripped him from Timber's grip and dragged him ten feet up the river in a single jerk.

"Erik's go-!" The transmission cut off as another tentacle wrapped around Erik's helmet, crushing the transmitter unit.

His weapon wouldn't fire underwater and he couldn't see a target anyway. The suit included three knives in easily accessible sheaths. Erik grabbed one of them and stabbed at the point where the tentacle was squeezing his head. The knife point slid along the armored helmet and then cut through dense tissue. It felt like rubber, resistant to the honed blade at first and then parting under the cutting pressure.

Another tentacle struck across the faceplate, sending Erik spinning in the current. Muted sounds of weapons fire burst through the water and then the tentacles withdrew. Erik struggled to find the right way up and crawled toward the bank.

II

The green-and-yellow mud was thick with grit. It scraped over Erik's faceplate and filled his view as he crawled out of the river.

Boots pounded past him, sinking deep in the mud. Weapons fire continued to burn the air and he heard the shriek of a trooper's pressurized suit being punctured.

Erik wiped the mud off his screen and regained his feet. The only sound was the ragged rasp of his own breathing and the muffled static of high-capacity weapons fire.

He lifted his rifle and saw the surface of the river erupting with grey tentacles that lashed out at the troopers on the bank as they worked to pull the wounded out of the current.

Erik joined the fight, going through the pre-fire checks of his weapon that they had drilled until he saw them in his sleep.

Slapping the safety into the KILL position, he sighted down the scope and opened fire. The caseless rounds tore through the exposed flesh of the beast. It was the biggest thing Erik had ever seen, and he needed it to die. Splashing into the river, Erik advanced in line with the rest of the squad.

Tracer rounds and exploding munitions sent chunks of grey flesh flying like clods of dirt. The creature's instinct turned to survival and it recoiled under the dark water. Erik kept firing until Mosan punched him in the side of the head.

Erik tapped the side of his helmet, the signal for comms damage. Mosan jerked a thumb over his shoulder to where the squad were regrouping on the right side of the river bank. Then he turned on his heel and walked away.

Timber approached and grabbed Erik's head. Twisting the damaged component release, he pocketed the dead comms unit and screwed in a replacement.

"You hear me now?"

"Comms check, Hey-Ho-Kay," Erik confirmed.

"Mosan is looking to strip you, man."

Erik nodded. Someone would be held accountable for any casualties. Mosan would ensure that the shit landed well downwind of him, and that meant the current squad leader was going to be held accountable.

Three bodies were retrieved from the river and two more were upright but supported as the squad hiked up to the camp site.

Mosan waited for Erik at the perimeter and then signaled him to step out and stand in front of the kill-sergeant.

"Your buddy clean the shit out of your ears?" Mosan spoke quietly. Erik flinched. He had never heard Mosan speak at anything less than a shout. It was a chilling sound.

"Yes, Kill-Sergeant!" Erik barked.

"How many troopers in Squad Cable?" Mosan asked.

"Twenty-two, Kill-Sergeant."

"Count them again!" Mosan's facemask clinked against Erik's as he yelled.

Erik executed a marching about-face. His boots striking up yellow dust as he turned 180 degrees. He scanned the survivors then turned back to face Mosan.

"Trooper wishes to report seventeen troopers operational and two wounded, sir!"

"Seventeen shooters and two zombies. Your little stunt decommissioned five of my squad!"

"Trooper didn't know there was a predator in the water, Kill-Sergeant!"

"Is that a fucking excuse!? Are you making a fucking excuse?!" Mosan grabbed Erik by the throat and shook him like a rag doll.

Erik rode it out. Mosan would scream and yell and then assign him a shit-duty as punishment. Eventually, it would be forgotten and he could go back to getting by.

"Stand there. Do not fucking move." Mosan walked away. Erik could hear him ordering the rest of the squad to set up shelters and stabilize the wounded.

After thirty minutes ticked by on the chronometer in his HUD, Erik wondered if Mosan had forgotten about him.

"Trooper Erik, about-face!"

Erik stamped his feet and turned in marching order. The squad stood in a line in front of the pop-up shelters. Mosan walked out in front of them.

"Squad Cable, you were twenty-five in number at the beginning of this training exercise. Casualties include Trooper Gilly, fractured ankle; Trooper Zooko, respiratory infection; Trooper Macowl, mental collapse. Three troopers dropped from the training exercise due to incapacitation. At no point during this exercise has anyone been responsible for the loss of life in the squad. Until now!"

Erik winced.

"Three troopers died today. Two more are wounded and will need to be vacked." Mosan reached the end of the line and turned back.

"Trooper Erik was designated squad leader. Trooper Erik ordered you shit-stains to get across the river. Trooper Erik failed to ensure the safety of the squad before proceeding into an unsecured environment. Trooper-fucking-Erik's actions led directly to the death of three of your squad."

Mosan turned and started down the line for a third time.

"We do not tolerate failure. We do not tolerate incompetence. We do not tolerate fuck-ups!"

The kill-sergeant turned and marched towards Erik. "You fucked up. You fucked up and people fucking died. You're going to have some time to think about how bad you fucked up."

Erik's rifle was taken away and Mosan dialed up a command sequence that gave him remote control of the trooper's suit environment. "Reducing life-support by eighty-five percent. You will remain exposed until we move out. If you are still alive at that time, you will wish you weren't." The suit's joints locked, holding Erik in a rigid standing position.

Mosan stepped back and then walked away. Erik felt the air warming in his suit, the stale taste of exhalation started to fog the faceplate. It would be dark soon. Outside of a tent, the temperature would plummet to well below freezing. With restricted suit function, staying alive would be a serious challenge. *They trained you to survive,* Erik told himself. *Do what you know.*

He worked on conserving the reduced oxygen, dozing while the light changed and darkness fell. The cold eventually woke him, and he shivered uncontrollably, unable to move or do anything else to keep his circulation going. His stomach rumbled with the rising need for food and water. He worked his mouth on to the nutri-tube. It was still sealed shut. Another function Mosan had shut down via remote access.

Curling his toes and fingers, Erik worked to drive the growing chill from his numb feet. The temperature continued to fall and frost started to form on the inside of his faceplate.

Red lights on poles winked in the darkness, marking the

sensor perimeter around the camp. If anything tried to approach, alarms would sound and the squad would come out of their shelters ready to kill.

What is your purpose? Erik asked himself. "To kill," he said aloud.

How will you achieve that purpose? "Be faster. Be stronger. Be better." *The fuck you say?* "Faster. Stronger. Better."

The mantra gave him a rhythm to tense and release his muscles. Faster. Stronger. Better. He imagined marching from perimeter pole to perimeter pole, straining to breathe in the thin atmosphere of his suit. In his mind, Erik marched up and down. How long had he been in the corps? Sixty cycles or six hundred?

Time meant little when he lived in The Mess, and once he passed through the airlock his life became a routine of eat, sleep, and run while getting yelled at. Mosan and the other trainers had one purpose. Make the recruits into killing machines or destroy them in the process. People dropped out and Erik never knew what happened to them. They didn't go back to life under the dome. No one who passed through the big metal door ever went back.

Everyone thought the volunteers went on to glory and a life of luxury. Now, Erik thought maybe they were killed, either in training or in the endless war against the Helos. The recruits knew two things about the Helos. First, they were the enemy. Second, troopers were the only thing that stood between the Diorites and utter annihilation.

If the Diorites were destroyed, then humanity would follow them into extinction. Erik was fighting for more than the slugs; he was fighting for Noshi and every other shit-eater in The Mess.

Noshi. He had to stay alive for her. Maybe she didn't care. Maybe she was dead.

Thinking of Noshi sent a fresh spasm of shivering rippling over his skin. The numbness crawled up his legs, and his fingers were dull as wood.

Being stripped, having his protective gear torn off so he could choke out in the acid gas atmosphere—that would be a quick death. Being exposed, locked in his suit, short on air and freezing to death. That wasn't a trooper's death. It was a shit-stain's way to die.

It got harder to breathe. Each dragging inhalation froze his face until Erik couldn't feel his skin. By the time his eyelashes were sticky with ice and he went back to sleep, he started to feel warm at last.

III

The flier skimmed through the mist, the controls adjusting automatically as the craft followed its pre-set course.

Noshi felt the subtle shifts in altitude and pitch through her seat. She waited in a state of metra, her subconscious expanding to encompass beyond the range of her physical senses.

Pizak's training was intensive, forcing Noshi to react and push herself into states of concentration she had never imagined. She studied sacred etchings, considered the finest examples of recorded *Ka'tharis* and found the wisdom in the symbols and accents of the ancient *Bwalla* archive.

In The Mess, songs and stories were passed on from generation to generation. The oldest stories were of the great expansion of humanity. Leaving the first world, colonizing and exploring a hundred other planets. The stories said the distance between people became too great and without a way of connecting with others across the void of interstellar space, humanity withered. Colonies fell to disease, disaster, or apathy. Entire populations destroyed themselves in wars over resources, beliefs, or ideology.

Then the Helos came, sweeping across the human systems and destroying everything they touched in their eternal war against the Diorites. Humanity lacked the resources and the will to defend themselves against the technologically superior forces who descended like wrathful gods.

After millions of years of evolution and progression, the

flame of humanity flickered its last and went out against the infinite backdrop of space. Only the glowing embers remained, a meager few taken in as refugees on the worlds of the Diorite Commonwealth. Given space under domes where the sulfur dioxide atmosphere was kept at bay and the air was the right mix of oxygen and nitrogen to let them live.

The war against the Helos was all-consuming for the Diorite Commonwealth. Suitable worlds for expansion and terraforming were hard to find, and the two ancient civilizations clashed with a cold savagery that would not allow either side to yield or show mercy.

Using humans to fight solved many problems for the Diorites. It allowed them to send troopers into worlds with atmosphere's toxic to the sulfur-dioxide breathing species. Worlds that, once the Helos were driven from the soil, could be claimed in the name of the Diorite Commonwealth.

Noshi felt the voices of the Diorites, a whispering murmur of a hundred billion minds. They communicated across vast distances, all minds able to touch all other minds. She was the only human they had found who could join them in the great choir of *Kashoun*. For Noshi, the song of creation was glorious.

Twenty seconds to target, the Diorite drone pilot reported.

"Gratitude for delivering me to my destination," Noshi replied with a smile. Among Diorites, emotion was the vehicle that carried the truth. Gratitude expressed, but not felt, would ring as hollow as a lie.

The flier settled on the dusty plateau, sending up jets of steam from the frozen crust. Beyond the swirling mist and Noshi's senses, the hab-tents glowed with internal lights. The flier transmitted a standby code to the perimeter defenses and Noshi made ready to exit the craft.

IV

Noshi sealed her suit and stepped out of the flier. The frosty ground crunched underfoot and she walked unerringly through the perimeter line and into the camp.

Turning her head, she sensed a fading life sign nearby. Human. Possibly a wounded recruit left to die. The hab-tents opened and the squad formed up in front of the new arrival.

"Squad Cable! Tenhut!" Mosan barked at the squad into formation. "Welcome, Herald," Mosan greeted Noshi formally.

"Kill-Sergeant," she acknowledged him in return. "Your squad is chosen. You are to return to the hub for to prepare for dispatch."

Mosan straightened, the pride in his voice evident as he acknowledged the order. "We obey the governor's command."

"How many casualties?" Noshi asked.

"Seven, Herald."

"There are sixteen recruits in the formation. The body over there still lives." Noshi waved to where Erik's still form lay in the cold dirt.

"Trooper Erik," Mosan explained. "Punishment detail for dereliction of duty resulting in the deaths of three squad members."

Noshi's mind reeled. *Erik?*

"Ha- Have that trooper loaded onto the flier. The command will wish to review his actions and develop control strategies to avoid such incidents in the future."

"As you say, Herald." Mosan gave the order on the squad comms channel. Timber and a second trooper sprang forward and lifted Erik's limp form from the ground.

"You are to return your unit to Hub immediately," Noshi said to Mosan. The kill-sergeant saluted to confirm the order was understood and accepted.

With her legs threatening to collapse under her, Noshi returned to the flier. She waited while the two troopers finished laying Erik on the craft's floor. Once they had stepped out, she entered and sealed the external doors.

"Cycle atmosphere," she said to the computer. "Set to human standard."

The air in the ship hissed and cleared. After a minute the console indicated the air was safe for her to breathe. Removing her helmet, Noshi crouched and felt for the sealing ring on Erik's facemask. Removing it, she let her fingertips flutter over his face. So cold... He was close to death, his breath barely whispering against her touch. "Increase atmosphere temperature by nine degrees."

With confident movements, she opened a medical kit and pressed a dermal infuser against Erik's neck. The device hissed and flooded his system with epinephrine. A moment later he gasped as his body flooded with adrenaline.

"Erik..." Noshi whispered.

"Am I dead?" he croaked.

"Not yet."

"Are you real?"

Noshi smiled in spite of her concern. "Yes, I am real. I was sent out to summon your squad back to the hub."

"Sent?"

"I will explain, in time. Right now, I need to get you medical attention."

"Medical?"

"You will live." Noshi stood, leaving Erik on the floor of the flier. Returning to her flight-chair, she ordered the pilot to lift off and in moments they were soaring above the yellow clouds under a star-lit sky.

V

Erik woke up in a warm place with filtered air flowing over his face. He could move his arms, feet, and head. Sitting up took a moment.

Plastic tubes and articulated tentacles tipped with dermal infusers surrounded him and his skin tingled where they had delivered their loads.

"Noshi..." Erik's throat felt clamped shut with dryness. He

coughed, feeling his throat scrape. "Noshi?"

"Herald Noshi is not present at this time." The voice came from somewhere.

"Where is she?"

"Herald Noshi is presently in conference."

"What does that mean?"

There was no response to the question. Erik set his feet on the warm floor and stood up, swaying until his equilibrium returned.

"Clothes?" Erik asked the empty room. A panel slid open and he crossed over, taking a familiar bodysuit from the compartment and slipping into it.

He turned to the sound of a door opening. Noshi walked in and regarded him in a slightly off-center way, as if she were listening to his presence.

"Noshi!" Erik resisted the urge to spring forward and embrace his friend.

"Hello Erik." Noshi smiled and moved into the room with confidence even Erik didn't feel.

"What happened?" Erik asked.

"In what context?" Noshi smiled. "What happened since you left the reservation dome? What happened since I was also taken into the program? What happened since I collected you from the field training exercise?"

"You look different," Erik managed.

"I am different. I have had an opportunity to learn a great deal. Much as you have."

"I've learned to kill, mostly." Saying it out loud left Erik feeling as empty as ever.

"You are a trooper for the Diorite Commonwealth. You fight for the safety of us all."

"People died because of me," Erik admitted.

"People will always die. What we achieve through their sacrifice is more important."

Erik wondered what had been achieved by the death of his squad mates. "Why am I here?"

"Context is important to Diorites. If you were to ask a Diorite that question, they would have no answer for you. You need to be specific."

"Right now, in this place. Why am I here with you?"

"I have the authority to make requests. So, I brought you back with me. It was preferable to leaving you to die in the wild."

"What do you do, for the slugs?"

"I am a herald for the Diorites. I assist them in matters of human interaction and strategic planning."

"Strategy—that's war planning."

"Yes, and so much more. The Diorite Commonwealth is expanding. More worlds are needed. They have taught you this as part of your training."

Erik nodded. "The Helos are our enemy. They seek to destroy the Diorites and the humans they protect."

Noshi dialed hot drinks from the food dispenser. "The Helos are a similar species to the Diorites. They breathe the same atmosphere and have the same metabolic processes."

Sipping his drink was easier than admitting to Noshi that he had no idea what she meant.

"Many suitable worlds can be terraformed to make them habitable for Diorites once the Helos threat has been eliminated."

"The slugs use us," Erik interrupted. "We fight the forces of the Helos for them."

"We are dependent on the Diorites for our survival," Noshi replied.

It was true. Without the Diorites providing food, oxygen and housing, humans would have died out long ago.

"I need to get back to my squad," Erik said. "Kill-Sergeant Mosan will want to finish punishing me."

"You are no longer under Mosan's command, Erik."

"I… I'm being sent back to The Mess?"

"No, Erik. You are being assigned to leadership training. In spite of your mistakes, you show aptitude for command."

"People died today," Erik reminded her. "Because I made a

mistake."

"As a leader, you will lose troops in battle. You will be trained to minimize those losses. You will be trained to ensure those losses are acceptable."

"Can they train me not to feel guilty?"

Noshi reached out and laid a soft, warm hand on Erik's. "You cannot know the truth of yourself."

"What does that even mean?"

"It means you will become who you are meant to be, in time."

"I'm not meant to be anyone. I'm a grunt, a weapon, a merc for the Diorite Commonwealth and when I die, they'll just call up the next starving kid desperate enough to do anything to get out of the shit."

Noshi's hand caressed Erik's arm. "I am on a path I never imagined. Things will become clear to you as you go forward."

"I'm crawling into darkness," Erik murmured, his attention on the soft touch against his skin.

The girl's smile was as brief as a blink. "You get used to it."

Erik flinched. "I'm sorry. That was wrong of me."

She slapped him hard and quick, the sting more surprising than painful.

"Never apologize. You must be strong and sure always. Anything else will be see as weakness. Perception becomes reality."

"You sound like Mosan."

"Your kill-sergeant knows the truth of war. There can be no mercy, no hesitation. You must be stronger and deadlier than anyone else. If you do not, the probable future will become uncertain, and without certainty we can never know victory."

"You sound like a slug." Erik scowled.

"They sense things beyond what mere humans can understand. I am learning from them."

"What happens when there are no more enemies? When the Helos are extinct?"

Noshi sighed. "There will always be enemies; it is the way

of war. If they do not present themselves, they will be created. Erik, I came to deliver orders to your squad. They are to prepare for deployment. Your training is complete Erik. Now you go to war."

CHAPTER 6

I

Sitting on a crate of supplies, Erik sucked on the nutri-tube and watched the newest volunteers stumbling out of their landing craft.

"Fuck me." Timber's voice spoke in Erik's headset. "Were we ever that clean?"

Erik grunted. Most of the new recruits would be dead by the time this world was claimed. Casualties were part of the reality of war. The trick was to last as long as possible.

A familiar computer-generated voice spoke in his ear. "Trooper Erik. Trooper Timber. Assignment."

"Receiving," they both replied.

"Reconnaissance team Argo-Typhon, to sector Kilo-17. Support armor platoon Echelon nine. Eliminate all enemy forces."

"Break time is over." Erik let the nutri-tube retract and stood up.

"Time to kill some mother-fuckers," Timber agreed.

They turned their backs on the fresh meat and shouldered their weapons. The standard trooper rifle fired a solid round the size of a man's index finger down a barrel ringed with electro-magnets. Each shot broke the sound barrier as it left the muzzle of the rifle. On full auto the blast of the rifle would chew through armor and shred anything organic.

The rifles were fitted with scope technology to assist accuracy and additional functions to transmit sensor data for orbital bombardment targeting and data uploads.

An experienced trooper of the Diorite Commonwealth in the right position could turn the tide of battle with this weapon.

They crossed the plateau where the Diorites had established

base camp eight hundred meters above the surrounding terrain. For the first week after Erik and his fellow marines had made planetfall, the sky had been streaked with vapor trails and the ground rumbled with the descent of supply ships bringing armored units, weapons, supplies, and construction bots down to the plateau. The rock underfoot vibrated as machines worked ceaselessly to strip anything useful from the landscape. First, they took the grass and trees. Then they mined the minerals buried beneath the surface. It was all taken up to the summit of the plateau where other machines used the raw material to print megalithic blocks of krete and construct defensive walls.

On the plains below, a network of excavation trenches provided defensible positions for the regiments of troopers fighting against the forces of the Helos. Erik's place was not behind such walls. He needed to face the enemy on his own terms.

Smoke and mist cast a dark pall over the torn ground. The only color were the rainbows on the surface of the hydrocarbon pools that filled the rutted tracks where tracked vehicles had stirred the dirt to mud. The armored units had rolled out an hour ago and were now closing on the enemy's last known position.

The two troopers filed onto a transport vehicle waiting to lift a squad to the battlefield below. The other troopers onboard nodded in respect as the two veterans took their slots in the standing frames. The carrier shuddered under power and lifted off, cresting the edge of the plateau before dropping into the swirling mist.

Erik listened to the sparse chatter over the comms. The 18th regiment were waiting for the latest Helos counter attack. Down there, a thousand men dug in to the mud and rock of Kursk Seven-A.

A marine's place was not behind such walls, and Erik's comrades were not part of the defenses. They were the assault forces of the Diorite Commonwealth who provided the machines of war while the humans provided the meat. It had been this way for longer than Erik had been alive.

Timber's life-signs dropped into sleep mode on Erik's HUD. His friend barely stirred when the rest of the armored squad thundered out of the tail end of the transport, throwing themselves into the meat-grinder of war.

II

This land had no name that Erik knew. One planet after another. Different atmospheres, different terrains, different environments. Some deadly, some not. All reduced to rubble and ashes by the carpet bombing of the orbital bombardment. Only when the Helos had been crushed did the human mercenaries land and begin the cleanup. The Helos themselves had usually moved on, leaving one or more of their soldier species to fight to the last in their name.

Erik waited until the exit light flared red and the clamps retracted from around his chest. He ran for the exit the way he always had. Charging into battle, ready to destroy any foe.

Timber's armored boots hit the ground a second after Erik's. The two troopers used the dust cloud raised by the hovering transport as cover while they ran to the shadows cast by a nearby ruin.

"Kilo-17?" Timber asked through a jaw-cracking yawn.

"Yeah." Erik crawled to the edge of a rubble pile and adjusted his HUD to scan the surrounding area. A city had stood here until recently. Now broken roads, destroyed buildings and drifting piles of wind-blown trash were all that remained.

Night was coming and the temperature dropped. Darkness meant different enemies—ones for whom the night was a natural environment and lived for the nocturnal hunt.

"Life signs," Erik reported. Timber slithered up beside him and waited while his sensors completed a matching scan.

"Check."

"Fucking Zaran," Erik murmured. The coiling serpent shapes rose out of the holes and cracks where they lay dormant during the day. Using the scopes of their rifles, the two troopers tagged each target for an orbital strike.

The first of the world's three moons crested the horizon, adding a sliver of reflected light to the deepening gloom. The Zaran rose on four thick tentacles that joined at a bulbous head. Each membranous sac was swollen with the slowly digesting remains of whatever life had built this city.

"Targets marked," Erik transmitted.

"Tagged and bagged," Timber confirmed. The troopers eased below the line of sight and made a careful retreat from the impact zone.

"We're clear," Erik reported.

"Orbital strike commencing." The soft feminine voice coming over the comms was computer enhanced. Diorites didn't talk the way humans did. They looked nothing like them, either, with their massive slug bodies and heads covered in meter-long tentacles that acted as sensory and communication organs. To Erik, the only thing uglier than a Diorite was whatever enemy the Helos threw at them. That voice would be the only warning they would receive. The missiles and rockets screaming down through the atmosphere were supersonic. By the time you heard the incoming shell, you were already dead.

Erik and Timber went to cover as the ground quivered with the first detonations. A kilometer away the surface erupted in a spray of mud and shrapnel. Fire burned the air and became smoke. The troopers watched the muffled flashes of the artillery inferno.

The visual sensors in Erik's faceplate HUD cycled through the electromagnetic spectrum. Depending on which species the Helos sent against them, and in the wake of the orbital firestorm, sensors scanning for body heat may not be a reliable way of detecting an incoming force.

"Clean and clear," Timber reported.

With Erik in the lead, they retraced their steps. Charred remnants of Zaran flesh were scattered among the freshly blasted rocks. The troopers didn't look for survivors.

"Map confirms Axander and armored unit Echelon Nine are

five clicks on bearing three-five," Erik announced. "We should check in on them."

"Coordinates locked in," Timber agreed. They kept walking, climbing over hills of broken rock and the local version of krete, their weapons sweeping the surroundings as they went. Being vigilant and ready to react instantly had kept them both alive for over a year in service to the Diorites.

Twenty minutes and three kilometers later, Erik signaled Timber to halt. "Movement."

"Got it," Timber replied. "Not Zaran," he added after analyzing the sensor data. "Could be Skivs?"

"It's not moving like the Skivs."

"You're a First Trooper. Fucking deal with it." Timber stated the obvious.

Erik would deal with it the way he had been trained. The same way they dealt with any foe when they made planet fall.

"All right, arm the fuck up!" Erik ordered.

A chill mist seeped from the ground and hid whatever shapes moved in the dark. There was no hiding from the scanning technology that detected heat, movement, and bio-electric signatures.

The glowing dots on Erik's HUD moved closer in a haphazard way, as if they were uncertain and without strong leadership.

"We should move in and destroy them." Timber spoke from his position at Erik's left.

"I'll know what the fuck I am facing before I destroy it," Erik replied.

"What does it fucking matter?" Timber came back. Erik's armored hands flexed into fists. *First Troopers do not respond to petty barbs issued by fellow troopers,* he reminded himself. Every instinct and his warrior's conditioning screamed that he should respond to the challenge and strike Timber down.

"We will know our fucking enemy," Erik said again. The Diorites had no military tradition that the humans could ascertain. Their rules were as simple as their training. Destroy the enemies of the Diorite in whatever form or location they were found.

The humans had developed traditions for war, passed on from training personnel like Kill-Sergeant Crysto and honed and sharpened in battle by troopers like Erik. Know your enemy meant being certain of your target before opening fire. There was no victory in killing your own.

"I'm First Trooper on this assignment, so you will not fire without my word," Erik advised. The order might have been unnecessary; for a battle-hardened veteran like Timber, weapon discipline was unquestioning. It removed any chance of failure. The responsibility of discipline was a circular thing. From Erik to the troopers he led and back to Erik. If they failed, then he failed. Even on a duo-mission like this, where the responsibility was shared with Timber, the accountability was Erik's.

"Cover positions. Be ready for anything."

Timber and Erik moved into place, hunkering down behind piles of rubble, the long muzzles of their rifles tracking the scattering of targets moving across their helmet screens.

Erik noted the lack of training in the movements of their targets. Whatever species approached, they were not an organized military force like the Skivs, the Ap'Aesh, or the reptilian Skurgen, all equal to the human forces in terms of supplied technology and training.

"Ten meters," Erik reported.

A breath of wind stirred the drifting smoke, and a shape drawn in dark stripes and muted colors appeared through the mist.

Not Skivs, Erik thought. "Hold."

A bipedal figure scrambled over the lip of a shell crater. It wore no armor and carried no weapon that Erik recognized. It seemed no larger than a child.

Sighting down his rifle scope, Erik hesitated. It was a child.

III

"Cover me," Erik ordered. The broken ground crunched under his armored boots as he walked out of cover and approached the child.

The small figure's face was dark with dust and grime, streaked with the tracks of tears and glistening smears of snot.

It wore no protection beyond the over-sized wrappings of filthy clothing and frayed boots. Erik knew the atmospheric makeup of the planet included a perfectly breathable level of oxygen, nitrogen and trace elements; there was no reason for the child to have protective gear. If anything, it confirmed his assumption that the young one was human, or close to it.

"SKIVS!" Timber bellowed across the comms channel. A wave of enemy force dropships crash landed a hundred meters behind Erik, and the Skivs came charging through the cover of drifting smoke.

The enemy stood over ten feet tall on thick legs supporting bodies protected by natural armor made of layers of chitinous shell. The faces of the Skivs were dominated by gaping mouths with long teeth, and their arms were twisted vines that could pick a single hair off the ground or pulverize krete with a punch.

Erik threw himself into the cover provided by the slope of the blast crater, grabbing the kid pushing it over the edge as he went.

Rising to one knee, Erik blasted the nearest Skiv. The enemy convulsed under the assault and kept charging. Long sinuous arms swung, and prehensile vine-like tentacles slammed into Erik's armor. The darkness and swirling mist shredded with the tracers of weapons fire as his aim was knocked upwards.

His suit's warning systems alerted Erik to the crushing power of the dark cords tightening around his chest. An enraged Skiv could crush a human in armor like they were an empty nutri-pac.

Fire flashed past in Erik's peripheral vision. An incendiary grenade flared yellow and orange, expanding like the sun and engulfing the skiv in burning fuel.

The grip around Erik's chest slackened and his air filters struggled to keep the worst of the stench of burning flesh out of his nose.

Shifting focus brought the next enemy into Erik's sights. He opened fire, aiming for the single least armored point on the towering Skiv. The super-sonic slugs tore into the thick bark flesh below the creature's head. In one long burst, the Skiv's head came off its shoulders and Erik snapped to the next enemy. There was no shortage of targets.

"Timber! Orbital strike! Target this position!"

"I ain't ready to die yet!" Timber snarled. He fired a steady blast of fire into the advancing ranks of Skivs.

Erik tossed a hex-charge into the advancing mob of Skivs. Fire was the one element that would break their attack. Erik and Timber brought the fires of Hell down on the surviving Skivs. A steady blast of weapon fire culled the ones who staggered through the spreading blaze of the incendiaries.

"Aseebee!" A woman's voice, loud and shrill with panic. Erik shifted his rifle to cover the direction of the voice. The larger figure scrambled over the pile of rubble, almost crawling on hands and feet as she rushed to gather up the child who lay huddled and screaming nearby.

The Skivs closed to melee range, the tendrils whipping through the air and kicking up dust and stones as they attacked. Erik fired a controlled burst into the charging form that filled his helmet view. Skiv vines curled around Erik's armor and alarms sounded, warning him that he was in danger from the pressure.

Erik's ears filled with a screeching howl as he fired again into the Skiv, sending splinters of Skiv bark flying through the air. His suit servos whined as the massive Skiv went limp and crashed against him.

"You gonna kill that thing? Or fuck it?" Timber asked over the comms between bursts of weapons fire.

With the crushing weight of the Skiv pressing him into the dirt, Erik strained to get clear. A hex-charge exploded close enough to tear the Skiv corpse away and send a hail of gravel raining down on Erik's armor.

Timber stepped up and extended a hand. "On your fucking feet, First Trooper."

"I'm up." Erik rolled to his feet and scanned the area. Chunks of bleeding Skiv were scattered across a battlefield silent except for the crackling of burning Skiv meat.

"Where's the fucking kid?" Erik asked.

"Who cares?" Timber kicked a Skiv head and sent it tumbling into the smoke before marching off in the opposite direction.

Erik switched his comms to external, "Kid!? We will not harm you!"

"Erik. Over here," Timber cut in.

On the other side of the crater ridge two figures were huddled together, skin gray with dust and ash.

"The larger one is showing life signs," Timber reported.

"Yeah." Erik's scans told him the same thing.

A human woman rocked the dead child against her breast.

"You should leave this area, it is not safe," Erik said.

"Yu koshi! Yu koshi casa meshen, ga-lo. Sou-ek, nakit tow!" The woman spoke gibberish to Erik's ears. He waited while his suit computer analyzed the language and attempted a translation.

"Go on, get the fuck out of here!" The broadcast voice turned his words into a close approximation of the language the woman spoke.

The woman scrambled backward, the child's limp body cradled in her arms. She looked around and stumbled over the crest of the rubble pile and hurried away.

Timber came striding over, his rifle leveling at the retreating woman's head.

"Hold!" Erik ordered. "Report file. Civilian presence. Human stock. Unregistered." The information was transmitted into the Diorite network. Many of the worlds they fought on were occupied with indigenous species. Some of those were sentient. This was the first time he had encountered anything that could be human.

"We continue to move forward. Recon pattern. Indigenous sentients' presence confirmed and reported. No indication of hostile behavior. Do not fire on un-sanctioned targets. Confirm."

"Confirm," Timber replied immediately. Erik put all questions of who the aliens were and why they were living on this world out of his mind and followed the woman over the crumbling ridge of the torn ground.

"Axander's last reported position is less than two clicks," Timber reminded him.

"My OPS is working just fine," Erik snapped.

"Unit Argo-Typhon, alert. A second wave of Helos forces are descending on your position." The soft feminine voice calmly warned them of impending death. "Four drop ships entering your airspace in three minutes."

Helos drop ships were simple and had minimum power systems to ensure they landed without destroying the fighter cargo. Beyond that, no one seemed concerned about how comfortable the gliders were. Erik had never heard of the Helos recovering landing ships. It seemed they were as disposable as the species they used to fight their long-running war against the Diorites.

"Do we have trooper support?" Timber asked. Erik relayed the question.

"Negative. All resources are currently allocated in other sectors."

"Assholes," Timber muttered. "That means no orbital strike requisition either?"

"You know that's how it works."

"We could take them on you know."

Erik grinned inside his helmet. "Be my fucking guest. I'll be sure to remember you next dead-day."

"Bitch, I'm going to drink to your memory at dead-days for so long, I'll be the only one who fucking remembers your whiney ass."

Erik's response went unsaid as he focused his attention on the terrain ahead. They skirted around a line of missile craters stitched into the remains of a road. Abandoned wrecks of what Erik assumed were vehicles were scattered along the roadway.

"More of your non-coms," Timber advised. He gestured at a cluster of decaying bodies in one of the vehicles.

"Zarans didn't come this far," Erik said.

"Maybe they didn't need to," Timber replied. "There's signs of habitation all over this area. The Zed's would have eaten all they wanted straight off the ground."

"You have more in common with them than you think."

Timber's barking laugh rattled through Erik's helmet and he kept walking.

iv

"Echelon nine, armor Command Axander, this is Recon team Argo-Typhon, copy?"

"Echelon nine, Axander, Copy."

"We are inbound on your position. ETA ten minutes."

"Roger that. See you in ten."

"If everyone was this welcoming, we would have won the fucking war generations ago."

"Maybe if you did your part," Erik replied.

"Shit, you'd be dead if it wasn't for me."

"Way I see it, if it wasn't for you, my ass would have been out of the fire more than it's been in."

The two troopers fell silent and walked as the second moon rose in a crescent sliver on the northern horizon.

"Argo-Typhon, this is Trooper Clix, we have you on our perimeter scans."

"Confirmed," Erik replied. The dust-marked bodies of the armored vehicles were arranged in a disjointed ring, ready to fire their heavy weapons in any direction.

A minute later they crunched the last few steps into the armored encampment.

"Welcome to sector Kilo-17." Axander stood in an armored suit that was a slimmer version of the ground troopers' gear.

Designed for the confines of the armored corp vehicles. it allowed easier movement at the cost of protection.

"You pick up any native lifeforms?" Erik asked.

"Nothing but Zarans, Skivs, and some random shit."

"What kind of random shit?"

"Small, and avoiding us. Which means not a priority for my unit," Axander replied.

"You didn't investigate?"

"What part of *not a priority for my unit* did you not understand?"

"We encountered unregistered human stock," Erik said.

"No shit?"

"No shit. Young kid and a woman."

"Where are they?"

Timber sighed. "The kid is dead. The woman took off."

Erik changed the subject. "You were notified about the Helos drop ships incoming?"

"Yeah. Not our priority either."

"Exactly what the fuck are you doing out here, Axander?"

"Well, trooper, we are winning the war for the Diorites."

"Great!" Timber cut in. "Does that mean we can go home now?"

"You can fuck off any time you like," Axander replied.

"Stand down," Erik ordered before Timber could escalate. "We have orders to provide recon support to this sector."

"Be my fucking guest." Axander leaned back against the armored flank of the tank and folded his arms.

"We need to resupply," Erik said.

Axander tapped his comms unit. "Clix! Front up!"

The side of the vehicle whirred and a hatch slid open. A trooper in the same slim-line armored suit as Axander stepped out.

"AC?" She broadcast on the open channel.

"Argo-Typhon are authorized for resupply. See to it."

"Aye, AC. Troopers, please step inside." Clix indicated the open hatch.

Timber went in, Erik on his heels. Axander reached out and caught him by the arm.

"Contact channel only. Trooper Erik, you need to understand. There's all kinds of life here. Just like on every other world the Helos have tried to fuck over. We don't focus our attention on them. We focus our attention on the enemy. Clear?"

"Clear," Erik snapped back. The civilian woman's anguished expression was still vivid in his mind.

CHAPTER 7

I

Erik's rifle vibrated against his shoulder as he fired a steady burst of metal into a charging Skiv. The giant jerked and spasmed as the slugs penetrated the natural armor and tore up the soft tissues inside. Erik moved to his next target as the creature collapsed at his feet.

The radio chatter had diminished to operational updates only. Erik maintained radio silence as Axander's squad didn't need him telling them what to do. Kill the enemy. Destroy them before they destroyed you. That was the only reason they stood on this broken ground. Erik knew that he and his fellow mercenaries would still be standing after the last of the Skivs had been eliminated.

A blast rocked Erik and sent a cloud of dust and grit boiling across the ground. His sensors cycled through the available spectrums to maintain his visual advantage. A Skiv blundered past, tentacle arms thrashing as it struck out blindly. Erik stepped aside and blasted the back of the creature's head until its dark blood splattered across his armor.

The servos in the armored joints of Erik's suit lifted his boots and he marched forward through the ruins of the city, firing his rifle as he came upon a new foe. Each shot found its target, punching through the organic armor of a skiv's back and decimating internal organs.

It was too late for Trooper Decoran. The trooper's bio readings flashed negative on Erik's screen. His limp body was lost from sight under the steaming corpse of the freshly killed Skiv.

"Clix, contact Echelon Nine. Artillery strike, Chaos Alpha Nugget. This position."

Ordering an artillery strike on their own position could be the death of the entire squad. Axander's armored vehicles were less accurate than the precision missiles of the orbital strike ships, but Erik had no qualms about the potential sacrifice. Destroying the enemy was all that mattered.

"First artillery strike inbound."

"Fight clear!" Erik ordered. He provided covering fire as the squad moved out of ground zero. They blasted the lumbering Skivs and ducked under the whip of their tentacle-like limbs.

For a moment, the atmosphere seemed to inhale, then the air and ground erupted in a hurricane of fire and shrapnel. Erik dived for cover, the roar of the exploding artillery drowning out all his system feedback. It would be a few seconds before he knew if any of his squad had survived.

II

The sun had risen and the all three moons were receding towards the horizon when a transport delivered two squads' worth of troopers. Erik and Timber were given new orders; each was to lead a squad in support of Axander's armored unit. Their focus was now on search and destroy of enemy technology and combatants. A quiet recon patrol was off the menu.

The air turned white with the atmospheric detonation of the incoming artillery. Erik's visor shields darkened and he relied on the vision generated on the interior of his helmet screen to guide him over the lip of a crater. A heartbeat before the shockwave hit him, he rolled into a gap in the rubble. The air folded and a great wind sent the krete and rocks around him spinning. The churn of dirt and rock tumbled over him with the dull roar of a series of explosions that vibrated through his armor and sent his organs quivering.

A vapor of anti-nausea medication misted in the interior of Erik's suit. He focused on breathing the metallic tang and let his equilibrium settle.

"Squad up," Erik managed. His visuals flickered and went dark. His suit had taken a shrapnel hit and the system was re-routing power and data channels through backup systems. It would take time to return and until then Erik was blind.

A long-buried sense of claustrophobia clawed at him. Erik tried to breathe, feeling his throat close in panic. The sensor feedback in his gloves cut out as the system prioritized the available power. He dropped his rifle and with tingling fingers he scraped at the locking ring on his helmet. It clicked and slid counterclockwise, releasing the interior pressure with a hiss. Erik slid the helmet off and took a shuddering breath.

The air tasted of burnt flesh and chemical smoke. A thick pall of dust clouded everything and he could see no movement. Rolling onto one knee, Erik scooped up his rifle. There were no skivs left standing. The dead were twisted and scorched, silhouetted by the burning hulks of their landing craft. The heat pulsed against Erik's exposed flesh and he swallowed hard.

"Fi... -roup. Coordinat-" The rest of the transmission was lost to signal weakness.

Erik stood, tapping at the earpiece of his comms unit. "This is First Trooper Erik. Repeat last."

"First Trooper Erik!"

He turned, the amplified voice came from Clix, her AV-suit stained with dust and enemy blood. A silver gash from a Skiv strike down her chest plate shone like a lightning strike.

"You are in breach of armor protocol!" By stating his offence, she was logging the incident with the data cloud, what the troopers called an R and R, *Received and Reported*. It would be investigated and if determined to be a valid demerit, his record would be updated.

"Helmet malfunction determined my action," Erik stated.

Clix strode down the scree slope of the crater and swept Erik's helmet off the ground. She thrust it at him, managing to express accusation through her blank visor.

"First Trooper Erik's helmet is malfunctioning," Erik stated clearly for the record and to make his actions formal.

"First Trooper Erik, receive my report. Four fatalities recorded: Kalban, Decoran, Quink, and Macco." Clix could have been on a training exercise for all the emotion in her voice.

Each dead trooper's suit would be broadcasting a retrieval signal to the orbital fleet. Erik had never been told where the bodies went. He hoped they found the peace denied them in life.

The survivors regrouped and conducted system inspections and repairs. Weapons were reloaded and Erik gave the order for a five-minute rehydration and nutrient break.

"Trooper Clix, authorized access squad leader protocol. Get me a system report on my troopers."

Erik wished he could suck on the feed tube in his helmet and wash the metallic taste of the scorched air from his throat.

The comms unit on his ear crackled. "First Trooper Erik, this is AC Axander. We are approaching sector Kilo-one-seven point four. Multiple heat signatures detected."

Axander's squad of armored vehicles were finding an alternative route through the worst of the ruins of the city. Erik assumed the city had stood for as long as the world had been inhabited. There was nothing left now, every structure reduced to rubble by the intense orbital barrage unleashed by the Helos and then the invading Diorite fleets.

The armored vehicles were not suited to the crumbling confines of narrow city streets with unstable ground over tunnels and any other cavities waiting to open and swallow them. Squads like Erik's troopers would be sent to hunt whatever living prey hid in the shadows.

"Identified?" Erik asked.

"No match on registered enemy designations," Axander replied. "It could be one of your natives."

"Command, First Trooper Erik will locate and detain humans for interrogation."

The comms fell silent for a second, then the impassive computer voice of the Diorite control responded, "Confirm. First Trooper Erik, proceed and identify. Detain unregistered human stock for analysis."

"Confirmed, Erik out."

"Confirmed. Axander out."

"Clix, get on the farsight, isolate any of those human stock heat signatures in range. Orders are to detain live specimens for questioning."

"Aye." Clix moved to obey. The trooper would be an excellent candidate for the lead position in her own squad. If she could lift her eyes from Erik's position as First Trooper long enough to prove herself.

Clix set up the observation post and monitored the scanner as it swept the area to a range of 3000 meters while the rest of the squad enjoyed the last minute of their R&R.

"Cluster of sigs, eight hundred meters, bearing one-twelve." Clix reported.

"Squad up, possible unregistered human stock. Eight hundred meters, bearing one-twelve. We detain for questioning. Confirm."

"Hup," the squad voiced their confirmation.

"First, orders if we are fired on?" Clix transmitted on the squad channel.

"Shoot to wound. Minimize casualties," Erik replied in kind.

"Hup," Clix confirmed.

The squad moved out, their armored boots leaving sharp prints in the dirt. The trail showed Erik's squad fanning out to cover a wider line of advance. They scanned the crushed buildings and rubble clogged streets ahead. The dying vegetation and rough ground left in the wake of previous assaults and bombardments gave little indication of what this place must once have looked like.

There had been no rain in the local area since Erik had been on world. The orbital fleet data service confirmed there were ten hours of remaining daylight and the forecast was for mild temperatures overnight, with clear skies. Tomorrow would be more of the same.

"Four hundred meters," Clix reported. Erik acknowledged her update with a curt "Hup."

Without his helmet, Erik had no HUD data to guide him. "Clix, update?"

"Pattern confirmed. Eighteen likely humans. Including juveniles."

"Our purpose is containment," Erik reminded the squad. They moved carefully now, following the contours of the ground and moving from cover to cover. For the first time since he left The Mess and donned the armored suit of a Diorite trooper, Erik saw the world without a helmet.

Erik waved Trooper Silian to the right. "Take a covering position ten meters," he ordered.

Silian kept low and vanished into the drifts of dirt and rock. Even though Trooper Silian had as much experience in war as Erik, he was on record as refusing promotion to squad leadership positions in the past. Erik figured that Silian would be leading the fight to victory long after he was dust.

"In position," Clix confirmed. The squad had reached their target points and waited Erik's orders.

"Squad, First orders. Do not fucking fire unless I command." Erik eased to a standing position and with his rifle cradled in his arms he started walking forward. Each step through the broken krete and loose ground made more noise than the entire squad had on their approach.

"Translation protocol," he said to his comms unit. "Standard speak to Kursk Seven-A. Unregistered human stock."

Taking a deep breath, he set his shoulders and called out, "Hello!"

The huddled figures sprang to their feet. Small children were scooped up by mothers and the men lifted rifles and other weapons.

"I'm a friend!" Erik's voice collected a strange echo as his words were translated into the neural net's estimate of the local language and amplified through the external speaker on his crippled helmet.

One of the males stepped forward warily, holding a gleaming length of steel sharpened to a razor's edge.

"Yu koshi!" the man shouted. *"Invader!"*

"No," Erik waved a hand, palm down in a left-to-right gesture. "Protector." The suit computer and attached comms unit had a direct connection with the entire Diorite network, and the computing power of that galaxy-spanning infrastructure was beyond imagining. Still, it would take more data to be able to communicate fluently with these people. If they proved to be of any value, they would be transferred to a containment facility like The Mess before the planet would be terraformed to suit the eternal Diorite Commonwealth.

The man's expression of stunned disgust required no translation.

"My name is Erik. We are here to help."

"Help?" the man turned and regarded the ruined city around them. "This is help?"

"The Helos, they did this. Not us. We came here to protect you from them."

"He-los?"

"Helos are invaders. They came from a world far from here. They find planets like yours and destroy all life. We are from the Diorites. We come to save your world."

"Why did the Helos come?"

Erik tried to shrug, but the gesture was lost in the suit. "I don't know. I only know what they do. I have seen it on other worlds. We have defeated them in other places. Saved people like yours. Made them safe again."

Silence fell over the group who watched from a few steps back. Erik let them consider his words for a moment. "What do I call you?"

"Malber-Chun," the spokesman replied.

"And you lead your people?" Erik asked.

"Sure, you could say that."

"This was your place?" Erik asked.

"This?" Malber-Chun looked around again. "This was a city of half a million people. A city of industry, businesses, schools, hospitals, museums, libraries, parks, and homes. Yes, you could say it was my place. It was everyone's place."

"We can help you-"

"Gasha you!" Malber snarled. The Diorite network tripped over a translation for the expletive. Malber kicked a rock and came charging forward. Erik tensed but remained still, willing the rest of the squad to hold their fire.

The man grabbed Erik by the collar of his armored suit and jerked him forward. "Take a fucking look at what your help has done! You came here and, with no warning or explanation, destroyed everything that we had!"

"Helos…" Erik said.

"Fuck the Helos. Fuck them and fuck you!" Malber pushed Erik back. His suit servos corrected and kept him on his feet.

"Yes! Fuck the Helos!" Erik yelled back. "And fuck the Skivs! And the fucking Zarans! And fuck this shit!"

Malber let him go, blinking in the face of Erik's fury as his words ran out and he howled in rage.

"Man, you are *peshan*," Malber laughed and clapped Erik on the shoulder. "What's a Skiv?"

"Big… ugly… fucking things. Armored with whipping arms and teeth."

Malber nodded, the humor draining from his face. "We have seen them. And a zah-rans…?"

"Big ball sack with four tentacles?"

"They bury themselves in the rubble and come out at night," Malber replied.

"Yeah, they come out at night. Mostly."

"We saw lights in the night sky. We thought it was a meteor shower until the bombs fell. Millions of people died. Our news networks showed us it was happening all over the world. Then, monsters landed and killed anyone left alive."

"How did you survive?" Erik asked.

"We hid, or ran. These are all refugees. Everyone one of us has lost friends, family, and *yakal*."

"What is yakal?" Erik asked.

"Waiting for something good to happen."

Erik waited, but the Diorite network did not provide him with a direct translation of the word. "We are looking for any alien technology. Places where the Helos have left equipment or built structures."

Malber gave a short, humorless laugh. "We see anything like that, we run like hell in the other direction."

"So, you have seen such places?"

"Yeah."

Erik waited for him to continue.

"I have seen my friends torn to pieces. I have seen my city destroyed. I have seen everything I have ever known turned to shit. But if some kind of base for these murdering fuckers is what you want to see, then sure, I can point you in the right direction."

"Clix, bring the squad forward. Real easy."

"Understood."

Erik's squad rose out of the rubble behind him. Their sudden appearance caused a wave of panic through the refugees.

"It's okay. They're with me."

III

"We're on track to rendez at those cords," Axander confirmed.

"Don't get too close," Erik replied. "We've got no visual on any enemy presence. Fuckers could be underground."

"If the scary aliens bother you, little girl, you tell me and I'll send in a salvo of big dicks. They'll drill down and detonate." Axander's sarcasm was to be expected. Weakness was despised in the corps, and Erik ignored the words.

Clix crawled on her belly to Erik's position. For someone who spent the war working a console in an armored vehicle, she seemed to be relishing eating dirt with an infantry squad.

"First," the trooper whispered.

"Hup?" Erik replied, not taking his eyes off the terrain ahead.

"I found a fresh slime trail, bearing two-forty."

"Zarans?"

"Either that or…" Clix trailed off, a suitable target for sarcasm missing from her vocabulary.

"Good survey," Erik replied. Timber would have told him at length how the slime trail must have been left by his mother, sister, or one of the hundreds of women that Timber was adamant he had slept with.

"File report to Armor Commander Axander. Update him on the cords. Request hold-fire until target verified. Hup?"

"Hup." Clix stood in silence for a minute, her report to Axander unheard outside her helmet.

Erik crept back from the surveillance point to where the refugees sat huddled under a bent sign that showed an image of a pair of smiling adults and two young children.

"Everyone okay?" Erik asked. The speaker on his damaged helmet echoed his words in the alien tongue.

Malber raised an empty nutri-pac in salute. "Thank you for sharing food."

Erik nodded staring back at the children who regarded him with wide, dark eyes. The edge of their hunger had been dulled for now, and with the children controlled, the adults would be more compliant.

"If you help us, we can provide more than enough food. Help us destroy the Helos and we can give you everything you need to rebuild your city." It was close to the truth and anything beyond gaining the native's trust was not Erik's concern. His duty was to the Diorite Commonwealth and the annihilation of the Helos.

"And if we don't want to help?"

"Sooner or later, something will kill your children. If they are lucky, they will be dead before they get eaten."

"You think you can scare us with words?" Malber tossed the empty nutri-pac aside.

"No."

"My family has lived for generations in this city. Then you

and your enemy came and we became refugees on our own land. You and your warriors should come with me. We will see if the others will listen to you."

"Squad, move easy. On me," Erik broadcast on the squad channel. Clix and the others came into view, appearing out of the dirt and falling into step on Erik's trail.

IV

"Your helmet is still not functioning, First?" Clix's question came on the hour, and the act of asking made it a report that would be filed.

"Your observation is correct, Trooper." Erik had the responsibility for keeping the squad alive. Clix knew if his equipment was faulty, then he may not be capable of fulfilling that responsibility.

"First Trooper-"

"Stand down, Trooper Clix. Your concerns are R and R."

She wouldn't let it go. Troopers like Clix would never let it go. When everyone was dead, her ghost would stand over Erik's corpse and remind him that he was at fault. This was as sure as the sunrise.

Clix spoke rapidly. "I could take a look at your faulty equipment."

"Thank you," Erik handed the cracked helmet over, his eyes scanning the broken skyline of the ruins. "Axander, you copy?"

"Axander here."

"Where are they taking us?"

"You're tracking to the center of the city. Sat recon has all kinds of ugly in those sectors. You're probably walking into a trap."

"A trap means enemy forces. Which is exactly where we are meant to be," Erik replied.

"Armor units are on course. We'll be with you ASAP."

"Erik out."

In formation, the squad followed the ragged line of Malber and his people.

"First, I have a question." Veteran trooper Silian had perfected the art of giving advice without calling you a dumb-ass.

"Speak," Erik replied.

"Orders are to detain any humans for questioning."

"That is correct."

"We don't know how many of them are in those buildings. We don't know their weapons status or their relationship with the Helos."

"The humans have shown no indication of hostility. The Helos enslave or destroy."

"This trooper recommends we proceed with extreme caution, First."

"Recommendation R and R'ed," Erik confirmed.

In the destruction ahead, the level of technology was hard to determine. Erik could see slabs of material similar to krete making up the broken walls of buildings. Walking through the rubble, they stepped over twisted girders of steel and their boots crunched glistening pools of shattered glass.

Malber and his group moved carefully, ducking under obstacles and pausing often to listen for any sounds. Erik kept his squad at an operational distance where they could engage the enemy without risking the civilians.

Everything Erik could see puzzled him. Before the ruin, the city must have been complex, with a grid of paved streets, and the remains of storehouses with goods now spilled on the ground.

"AC Axander, Erik, copy?"

"Copy."

"Helos ship inbound on your cords."

Erik waved his squad to a halt. They dropped immediately, taking cover and following the trajectory of the alien craft as it whooshed overhead before vanishing into the darkness.

"Where are the fucking civilians?" Erik asked. He mentally

kicked himself for losing them in a few seconds of distraction.

"Bearing ten-five. They went to cover." Clix gave her report like she was on the testing ground in the training dome.

"Squad, find cover and maintain a secure perimeter. Clix, Silian, on me." Erik took the lead, sweeping the area with his rifle as he went in search of Malber.

Ducking under a tilted slab of krete, Erik activated the flashlight on his rifle. A narrow tunnel sloped down into darkness and the walls had been marked with unreadable symbols. The unfiltered air was strange to Erik, and he sniffed before stepping into the darkness.

V

"First, we should hold and report" Clix was regurgitating the basic training ops procedures that had been drilled into Erik a lifetime ago.

"Clix, you can stand the fuck down or you can shut the fuck up." Erik mentally scolded himself as soon as he had spoken. A First Trooper should encourage adherence to regs at all times.

"First?" Clix couldn't keep the surprise from her voice.

"Quiet, Clix. We're working here." Silian had earned the respect of other troopers the hard way and Clix remained silent.

Erik stepped out into a domed chamber, dotted with makeshift shelters and the glow of more smokeless fires. Malber stood near the entrance, the rest of his group had gone further into the settlement.

"I would see the faces of those who follow you, Erik," Malber announced.

Several other men and women moved closer in the gloom. Some carried rifles of a simpler technology than Erik's Diorite-issued weapon.

"It is against our laws to remove our armor when in battle."

"There is no battle here," Malber replied. "We are the dead left behind."

Erik scanned the gathering figures, looking for signs of hostility and immediate threat.

"First, recommend you advise civilians to back away." Erik

could hear the unease in Clix's voice.

"Trooper Clix. Head back up the tunnel. If you start shooting in here, we will lose an opportunity to gain valuable intel," Erik said.

"First, I-"

"Move, trooper," Erik broke in. He didn't have to turn to see her heading up the tunnel. Instead he stepped forward into the flickering circle of light.

"See, I am just like you." Erik spoke into the throat mic on his headset. The helmet picked up the signal, translated it, and his voice spoke in a garbled echo.

"You are nothing like us." Malber walked through the ranks of the gathered Kursk humans. "You can go deeper, or you can return to your masters."

The crowd parted to allow Erik through. Silian remained resolute and unmoving at the mouth of the tunnel.

"How many of you down here?"

"Why do you care?" Malber didn't look back.

"We need to know so we can provide food, medicine, shelter."

"We have all those things."

"We can give you back your world," Erik insisted.

"I told you, it is not yours to give."

Erik fell silent. There were protocols to gaining the support of native populations, though such things were not part of his training. This was the first time he had spoken with a native of any the war-worlds, and he had run out of standard things to say. "You're right. I have nothing for you."

"Come, eat with us." Malber led the way.

*

"Confirm your last?" Timber said.

"First Erik followed a group of natives into an underground space. He hasn't returned to the surface," Clix repeated.

"Status of the squad?" Timber asked.

"Kalban, Macco, Quink, and Decoran were terminal casualties. Trooper Silian went with First Erik. The rest of us are secure, sector kilo-one-seven."

"Have you reported to Armor Commander, Axander?"Negative, First Trooper. I... First Erik is your peer. I thought it prudent to contact you first."

Clix heard Timber's teeth grind together over the comm link. "Hold your position. First Timber, out."

The communications line clicked off and Clix allowed herself a deep breath. First Erik and First Timber were veterans of the war. Whispers around the platoon suggested they had been in service for more than five standard years. To fresh troopers like Clix, with less than three months' battle experience, they were old men.

In Clix's mind, old men were dead wood; they needed to be cut away to make room for new growth. Troopers like Clix who would lead the squad the way it should be run. The Diorite Command would reward her service.

Of course, they would hold Erik accountable for his actions and if Timber did not denounce his friend, he would also be liable. Either scenario meant victory for Clix.

CHAPTER 8

I

Noshi…

A caress across her consciousness gentle enough to bring her attention without disruption. In response, she visualized a blooming flower of primary colors that contained the knowledge of worlds in each petal. Releasing the vision expressed acknowledgement.

Pizak.

A report has been received. The one coded Erik has stepped away from the path.

Noshi focused on exercises of control, maintaining the cyclic flow of the brightly colored bloom in her mind. Reports on Erik's situation had been hard to come by in the steady flow of data pouring in from every corner of the war. She knew that he was alive and had proven himself an effective soldier in every theatre of combat. That Pizak had deemed it necessary to isolate Erik and advise her of the consequences of his actions filled her with a very human curiosity and unease.

Noshi gathered her thoughts. *I confirm my understanding.* The visual display communicated in ways beyond mere words.

It is accepted that your time here has come to an end. The way ahead is yours to create from the endless probabilities of the dimensions.

Pizak? Noshi could not keep her surprise hidden. Being blind since birth meant she had a perspective on the world that was different from others'. The concept of color had confused and elated her. The Diorites communicated amongst themselves and with her through their mastery of the full range of the electromagnetic spectrum. Through intense study, Noshi had learned the Diorite techniques that distilled the essence of thought until it could be projected into a receptive mind. The recipient's interpretation was as much a part of the communication as the initiator.

You are the Herald. You will be recorded as such in the sacred Bwalla. *Noshi, an eternal hub in countless probabilities of ka'tharsis.*

Noshi sorted through a multitude of questions. *I will feel your presence again.*

Pizak's mental touch was like a gentle hand on her shoulder. *Study the probabilities. All things are possible in the expanding Universe.*

Then she was alone.

II

"Sorry there isn't more. We haven't had a chance to go to the store," Malber said between shoveling spoonsful of stew into his mouth.

"I've eaten worse." Erik had never sat down to eat with aliens before. Even ones that were of human stock. Such a thing was a breach of protocol.

"The juice in bags?"

It took Erik a moment to realize that Malber was referring to the nutri-pacs they had given the refugees earlier. "Zarans like underground spaces. They will be attracted by the warmth of so many bodies."

"We have fought them off a couple of times already," Malber shrugged.

"They will come back and with others. The Helos will not stop until you are all destroyed."

"And you and your people? You won't stop until these Helos are destroyed?"

Erik nodded. "It is our purpose."

Malber set down his cleaned plate and stared into the flickering glow of the small fire. "There was a time in the history of my people, after victory in battle, we took others as *ebad.*"

"What does that word mean?"

"*Ebad?* It means servant. Specifically, a person who works for another without payment."

Erik wondered why the Diorite network could not provide a translation to the word.

"There are people alive today—well, people alive recently—who remember those days. The ebad were treated like animals. They had no rights, could own no property and had to do exactly what they were told, when they were told. Times changed. Those who owned people came to see them as human and the practice was outlawed. When it was made law that no person could bind another without payment or rights, the ebad were upset. We do not want to be free, they said. When the lawmakers asked them why they did not want their freedom, the ebad told them, Without our servitude, we have nothing. It is our purpose."

The two men sat in silence and Erik waited for Malber to continue.

"How does the story finish?" he asked eventually.

"That's it," Malber said with a half shrug.

"Okay." Erik went back to watching the flickering shadows beyond the firelight.

"You don't have any thoughts on the story?"

Erik frowned. "The rulers changed the way things were. It is what rulers do."

"This is true," Malber nodded. "The ebad, they had never known anything but servitude. When they were offered freedom, they were afraid."

"That makes sense. Why change the way things are meant to be."

"Things are not meant to be that way. People are not meant to be ebad. No man should have such control over the life of another."

Erik's hand caressed the flank of his rifle in an almost unconscious gesture. "With this rifle, I control the lives of many. With my training and rank in the ranks, I control the lives of every trooper under my command. That is the way things should be."

"Man, you are *ezayen*." Malber chuckled and his tone suggested it was the kind of putdown Erik expected from his comrades.

"I need to get back to my squad." Erik stood. "Thank you for the hot food."

"You know how they convinced the ebad to leave their masters?" Malber asked.

"Is it part of the story?"

"The law makers went to the ebad and told them that if they accepted their freedom, they would be given everything they needed to stand alongside their former masters as equals."

"That would make sense," Erik replied.

"It worked. The ebad walked away from the homes they had known, the families they had grown up with, the fields and factories they had worked. In return, they were given houses of their own. Jobs and education. Everything their masters took for granted was given to them."

"I will come back with support personnel. Medical supplies, food and better defenses." Erik headed towards the exit.

Malber watched the trooper go. His father had been the first-born child of ebad parents when they were given their freedom. Malber heard the stories from his father. After their freedom, the ebad were crammed together in cheap and segregated housing. Crime escalated, and they found themselves competing for jobs that they had previously done by birthright. Sickness and drug abuse became a problem. Within a generation, those who had been ebad were lost and dying. People like Malber's parents were the lost generation. The outcome of a social experiment in freedom that had unfortunate side effects.

Not that any of it mattered anymore.

A woman took a seat next to Malber at the fire.

"I am sorry for the loss of your son, Sara-sha," Malber said, his eyes fixed on the low flames.

"Thank you. I will not allow my grief to compromise our work."

"Do not allow our work to compromise your grief," Malber countered.

Sarah-sha wrapped a dusty wrap tighter around her shoulders. "I do not believe it is wise to allow the outsiders to much contact with us."

"I agree, Sara-sha. We knew this day would come and we have prepared for it. We will continue digging. Once we reach the temple, we will be free."

III

Silian glanced back as Erik approached. The trooper's silhouette fading against the dying light of the day.

Erik sank down and scuttled to Silian's side.

"Stat-rep," he ordered.

"Second Helos ship came in. Same landing cords. We have forty-five minutes of light remaining."

"The others?"

"They have followed orders." For Silian, following orders was a statement of fact.

"Hup. Let's move." Erik broke cover and headed up the tunnel to the surface, Silian following on his heels.

They took cover at the surface, waiting and watching like timid burrowers, scanning for predators before leaving their nest.

"First Trooper Erik. Clix, you copy?"

"Copy." Clix's response was immediate and crisp.

"First and Silian are on track. Confirm lock."

"Shall I transmit cords to your HUD?" Clix asked.

"Neg. The trooper is aware that First Erik's HUD is snaff."

"All troopers must maintain equipment in operational state. If a trooper is unable to ensure operational status of equipment, trooper may be required to relinquish squad position or be re-assigned."

Erik reminded himself not to respond. Not to lose control. Not to show weakness.

Silian tapped him on the shoulder and pointed with a gloved hand into the deepening gloom. Erik silently cursed his damaged helmet and squinted at the shadows. A shape moved between to spires of broken wall.

"Squad, First Erik. Eyes on Zaran. Silian, transmit cords."

"Received," Clix replied a moment later. "We are inbound."

The Zaran was larger than the usual troops. From tip to tip, its tentacles spanned twenty meters. Erik watched the thing as it lifted itself up and moved to their right.

"Clix, be advised. Eyes on Zaran that is bigger than I've seen before. It's gonna be a shit to put down."

"Received and understood." To survive, Clix would have to prove herself in battle as Erik and others had done before her. Erik waited to see what she would do next.

"AC Axander, First Erik. Copy?"

"First Erik, copy."

"We are almost on you. Request stat update."

"Zaran on our sight line. A big one. Advise two Helos ships landed half-click ahead."

"Confirmed. Your call on art strike."

"Confirmed. Hold for art strike coordinates and go. I say again, hold for go." The comms channel clicked off. Erik watched the Zaran moving until it was almost out of sight.

"First Erik, Trooper Clix, copy?"

"Trooper Clix, copy."

"What is your attack plan?"

"First?" Clix couldn't keep the surprise out of her voice.

"Trooper Clix, you are lead on squad until we regroup. What is your attack plan?"

"First, I…"

"Target is moving on vector oh-nine, trooper. What is your attack plan?"

Clix hesitated for a moment. "First, squad will move to engage in pattern rome-e-oh. Request orbital strike on target cords."

"Negative on orbital. Assets are out of strike window. Try

again, Clix."

"Armored Command. Uh, request AC Axander provide artillery support."

"Trooper Clix, contact AC Axander. Advise target cords and target specs."

Erik listened in silence as Clix made her transmission. Axander's response came through his headset.

"AC Axander, art request confirmed. Holding for go."

"Trooper Clix, AC Axander, you are go for art strike."

"Neg on strike command, Trooper. First authorization required for go," Axander replied.

"First Trooper Erik to AC Axander. Adjust strike cords, zero point four on bearing zero-nine. You are go for art strike. I say again, you are go for strike."

"AC Axander, copy. We are go for strike."

Silian sank into a crouch as the deep cough of the armored command weapons firing echoed across the broken city. Erik remained standing until the flash lit the sky. Then he dropped and hugged the ground that rippled like water with the detonation of high-explosive shells.

IV

Debris fell like hailstones, pattering across the ground in a swarm of disembodied feet. Erik covered his head as the raining shrapnel struck him and drew blood.

"Stand by for visual," Erik transmitted. Standing, he moved forward through clouds of swirling smoke and choking dust. The artillery barrage had left a field of craters, and chunks of Zaran meat quivered in the dirt.

"First Erik, AC Axander, visual confirmation of effective strike. Target nuked."

"Copy."

"First, squad regroup at strike cords."

Silian and Erik marched over the churned ground. The

remaining members of the squad came into view, moving in the recon pattern Clix had ordered.

They walked through the drifting smoke, Erik and Silian taking their positions in the squad formation and covering their points.

"What is that?" Clix broke radio silence, and Erik was too surprised by the view to reprimand her. In a freshly ploughed field pitted with impact craters, the remains of alien structures and ships burned.

Erik had never seen a Helos troop encampment. In his experience, all of them, from the lumbering Skivs to the tentacled Zaran, were a mobile force. Dropped to the surface of a planet in great numbers, they attacked everything around them until they were destroyed or recalled.

Something had been built here since the orbital bombardment had destroyed the city. The ringed complex of low structures and high defensive walls looked entirely different to the surrounding ruins.

"First Erik, AC Axander, you copy?"

"AC Axander, I copy."

"The Helos were building something there."

"Hor'shit."

"I'm certain." Erik watched the ground carefully. Too many of his troopers had been taken by vanguards of Zaran buried in the earth after an artillery barrage. "What's your ETA?"

"Open your ears, First. We are on approach."

Erik didn't bother reminding Axander that his helmet with its range of sensors and HUD readouts was hanging, cracked and dead, from his belt.

After a few seconds of intense listening, he heard the grind and whirr of the armored vehicles closing in. "Clix, confirm approach to Armor Commander Axander."

"Hup," Clix replied.

The squad moved into position, taking cover in the nearest shell craters. The armored bulk of the tanks crested the rubble and drove down into the smoking remains of the Helos encampment.

"Would you look at that." Axander sounded amused. It was the closest he would come to admitting that Erik was right.

"We have to report this," Erik replied.

"Uploading full sensor sweep to the network now."

"Squad, any movement?" Erik raised his head and gave the land ahead the once-over as his squad reported back in the negative.

The armored artillery vehicles rolled to a halt, puffing steam as their drive systems vented heat against the dark ground. Where the vapor hit the churned-up dirt, something moved and Erik shouted his warning a moment too late.

Under the right track of Axander's armored vehicle, the ground liquified, dropping the heavy machine on its side. A gelatinous goo flowed up over the armored panels and quickly engulfed the rest of the machine. Erik's squad opened fire immediately, their steady blast of rounds doing nothing to stop the flow.

Axander's vehicle fired its weaponry. Flashes of light and the burning heat of superheated plasma melted the ground to dark glass.

In seconds, the tank was dragged underground, leaving a geyser of mud spraying skyward in its wake as the weapons fire continued to rend the dirt and the air.

Erik ignored the screams and chatter filling his head piece with noise. Across the bombed ground other pits opened up and the remaining vehicles were swallowed whole by massive, amoeba-like forms.

"Squad, pull back! Pull back!" The vehicles were lost and this enemy could not be harmed by rifle fire and grenades. Erik waited till the last of his people had retreated outside the crater rim then followed them.

"What the fuck was that?!" Clix demanded.

"Your enemy," Erik replied.

"AC Axander! Do you copy!?" Clix ignored Erik and transmitted on the open frequency.

Erik strode over to where she stood and wrenched open the seals on the trooper's helmet. Pulling it off, he exposed Clix; Straight black hair and dark eyes filled with terror and shock.

"Are you afraid, Trooper Clix?"

"Axander and the others—they are gone!"

"Yes. They are dead. You are alive. You want to die too?"

Tears welled and fell across Clix's cheeks. "No, First Trooper!"

"Then remember your dead. If you want to honor them, remember your training. Remember your enemy. And most of all, remember your hatred. Fuel your inner fire with it. Unleash that anger that grief and that fear on each enemy you find. Kill them with your rifle. With blades. With rocks. With your fucking bare hands if you must. But do not let your friends die for nothing!"

Clix's face went still as if a mask had slid down. "I understand, First Trooper. I will know the enemy and I will kill the enemy."

Erik nodded; he had seen this before. The moment when the inexperienced broke through the wall of their fear and at last became soldiers.

He handed the trooper's helmet back to her. "You'll get your chance soon enough."

V

The vast distances between stars were an obstacle humanity had only managed to conquer by traveling at speeds close to the absolute of light. Generations were kept in a hibernation close to death for hundreds of years as they crossed the dark void between stars with the dream of arriving on a new world and making it their own.

Many did not arrive, destroyed by debris impact and systems malfunctions. Or they simply disappeared.

Those that did put down roots and became the seedlings of

the expanded human civilization. Over centuries they spread from star system to star system, refining their technology and embarking on what the optimists foresaw as a new golden age for the species.

Then humanity made contact with the Helos and their extinction was unavoidable.

Noshi isolated the feelings of grief and loss washing over her. The data stream filled her senses, sensations and noise. Light and ever-changing patterns. All of it revealing the past and, if analyzed closely, probabilities for the future.

Pizak would disapprove of her emotional response. But he was distant from her now, and she flowed in the embrace of the network. Her physical form reduced to data that would fill a fresh version of herself at her destination. The thought did not concern her. Pizak had taught her the truth of energy; everything was energy. It could be transformed, reshaped, and transferred, but never destroyed.

As energy she had been transformed and now transferred across light-years from Pizak's world to one of the front lines of the war against the Helos.

Pizak called her the Herald. One who would be remembered in the *Bwalla*, the Diorite archive of all knowledge. Her future actions would have an effect.

CHAPTER 9

I

You are coded, Noshi.
I am.
The probability of your arrival was indicated by Pizak.
He has been my teacher and guide.
Do you have understanding of your purpose.
I do.
Rise and be Noshi.

Noshi sat up slowly. Her limbs felt familiar and strong. She found the darkness comforting, blinking a couple of times to assure herself they had not restored her sight in this replication of her body.

Clothing has been prepared to suit your form.
My gratitude.

Noshi felt along the edge of the soft bench she had lay on. Fabric, familiar shapes of clothes and boots. She dressed and took stock of her surroundings.

The room was identical to the one she had left—when? A second? A year? She had no reference for the time of her travel, so she dismissed the speculation.

Without appetite, Noshi ate food from a dispenser, identical in function and texture to her last meal. After eating, she meditated, bringing to mind the lessons Pizak had taught her and always seeking further wisdom.

I am Kulf'k
I acknowledge you, Kulf'k.
It is accepted that you will leave this facility now. Transport to the planetary surface awaits you. It is understood you are skilled in the operation of mechanical transportation.
I have been trained.

Relocate as you will.

Noshi felt the light touch of the Diorite's consciousness retreat and once again she was alone. She took a few moments to put away the thoughts and mediation patterns laid out in her mind. Only when she was conscious and fully aware of her surroundings again did she move toward the door.

Navigation through Diorite structures required her to use the knowledge gained through long hours of intense study. While the Diorites had evolved to utilize a range of sensory organs, Noshi had always been blind and for her, touch, sound, and scent were her primary detectors of the world.

A sense of enhanced probability guided her around a corner. She felt the presence of many Diorites ahead, though they chose not to acknowledge her, for which Noshi was grateful. To exchange with so many would be distracting.

She entered a vast chamber and walked down a row of shuttle vehicles. They were shaped in various sizes, each for a different purpose. She hesitated when the probability seemed strongest.

I am to pilot this vessel.

This is confirmed.

My gratitude.

Noshi ran her hand along the sleek flank of the craft as she walked its length. It felt the size of similar craft she had flown with room for a single pilot and scant space for anything else.

The hatch on the ship opened at her touch and she ducked inside. The vehicle hummed and the automated systems guided her out of the hanger and into a vast emptiness. Patterns swirled in Noshi's mind; she focused on the references to Erik.

Pizak could give her no directive. He had provided her with the data and training to interpret the inherent probabilities across a universe of potential futures.

Noshi often questioned if her actions were her own, or were the probabilities were pre-determined? Pizak had no answer, guiding her to focus on the interplay of Ka'tharsis and the endless kaleidoscope of probability.

The lack of certainty always left Noshi feeling unsettled. She needed a final truth to be discoverable at the summit of her journey. Why else would she keep going?

Feedback through the ship's systems confirmed she was in a static position between a much larger craft and a planet.

Imaseru, the moment before change. Pizak would tell her that this was only detectable in hindsight. Noshi felt the weight of imaseru pressing in on her from all sides.

With a deep breath, Noshi opened her mind to the data flow, filtering out everything irrelevant to Erik's location. She took the coordinates of his last recorded position and guided the small ship into the dense atmosphere of the planet.

II

The ground shuddered underfoot, convulsing and rising up in a series of cracks and steaming fissures.

"Erik, you asshole. What the fuck is happening in your sec?" Timber was almost laughing over the comms.

"Serious shit," Erik replied. The blasted range where the armored vehicles had been swallowed was filling up with a biological mass. To Erik it looked like the same creature or form that had dragged Axander's vehicles and crew to their deaths.

"The net is reporting a localized seismic disturbance." Timber reported.

"Sounds about right."

"You have eyes on AC Axander?"

"Negative. AC Axander is down. Repeat, AC Axander is down."

"Well shit."

"Yeah."

"My squad is ee-tee-ay ten. If you need us to wipe your noses and dry your fuckin' tears."

"By all means, come over and see how it a real trooper wins the fucking war."

Timber did laugh that time. "We are inbound."

Erik ordered his own squad further back. The amorphous mass rising out of the ground had stopped swelling. The glistening surface seemed to be crystalizing as it dried in the air.

"Silian." Erik summoned the experienced trooper to his side.

"Yes, First Trooper?"

"Have you ever seen anything like that before?"

"Negative, First Trooper."

Erik nodded. "We pull back another hundred meets and maintain surveillance."

"Hup." Silian stepped back and shared the order with the rest of the squad.

Erik headed into the shelter of the dead city, his squad spreading out around him. When he stopped, they started digging in.

By the time the daylight had faded to gray dusk, Timber's squad had arrived and their combined forces were dug in and maintaining a watch on the dome.

"What the fuck is it?" Erik asked.

"You know, from here, it looks like a big bubble of snot," Timber observed.

"What the fuck is it?" Erik asked again.

"Sensor network is still gathering data."

Timber held out Erik's helmet. "I fixed it. You should put it on. No point in letting everyone see how fucking ugly you are when you cry."

"Thanks and fuck you." Erik took the helmet back. Only a few hours breathing unfiltered air and he was loathe to seal himself away again.

Timber's helmet stared at Erik until he sighed and slid it over his head. The locking ring slid into place and his suit re-pressurized. The HUD screens flickered and began to relay data. Squad updates, local terrain scans, data network feeds, all filling his senses with information. Erik felt like he had stepped into a crowded room after spending a day alone in the wilderness.

"All good?" Timber asked.

"Affirmative," Erik replied. "This is reconnaissance team Argo-Typhon to Delta-Nova-Alpha. Requesting sensor sweep update on unknown biological."

"Data processing," the computer-generated voice of the Diorite Commonwealth replied.

"Let me guess, the bitch said data processing?" Timber cut in.

"Yeah."

"I'd like to give her some data to process."

Erik scowled and waited for an update in silence.

"We can wait for the network to update, or we can go ahead and win the war," Timber suggested.

"Right, we should get some eyes on," Erik signaled the unnecessary screens to close on his HUD and crawled out of cover, Timber sliding in the dirt behind him.

Together the two recon troopers edged closer to the rising snot bubble.

"It looks like some kind of krete matrix," Erik said.

"You think they spray it out in liquid form and it cures in the atmo?" Timber asked.

"We've seen freakier shit. Cover me, I'm going to get a sample for analysis."

"Lookit you, goin' all tech-badge and shit."

Erik didn't reply. Neither he or Timber had qualified for anything more specialized than recon and killing the enemy. They had both seen humans working in technical. How they had been trained or assigned was a mystery to Erik. He had his own skills and so far, they had kept him alive.

Crawling up to the lip of the crater, he used his suit sensors to scan the material close up. A pale, sponge-like material formed a diamond-shaped lattice. Each pane was filled with a translucent film. All the readings confirmed it was biological in origin.

Erik poked the film with a gloved finger. It held with a rubbery resistance. Reaching down, he slid a knife out of his boot and pressed the gleaming tip against the film. It cut through and the helmet sensors warned him of a gas oozing through the gap.

"Timber, this shit is pretty soft. It cuts easy."

"Copy that."

A slice was quickly stored in a container and sealed for transport to the orbital fleet.

"Don't move." The casual tone had gone from Timber's voice. Erik froze.

A shape moved on the other side of the dome—a Zaran with tentacles coiling around its spherical body. With a wet slapping sound, a tendril smeared over the hole, sealing it with a glistening goo.

Erik waited until the shape slithered out of view.

"I think it likes you." Timber grinned.

"Fuck you," Erik replied, feeling the tension ease out of his muscles.

The dome glistened under the last light of the setting sun, Erik and Timber remained still and waiting until full dark.

"First Trooper Erik?" Clix came online.

"Go ahead, Clix."

"I am receiving a message from the orbital command. They require you to know that a ship is coming down to the surface."

"Advise, message received." Erik wondered what they had discovered for the Diorite Commonwealth to send a ship down from the orbital command fleet so quickly.

The small shuttle craft came into view, sweeping over the dome and angling in a wide circle above the troopers dug into the ruins.

Erik relied on his sensors to track the ship as it came in to land with a roaring hiss that sent dirt and debris swirling into the night sky.

"Single pilot craft, DC authorized," Erik transmitted to the troopers on the ground.

"They must want this bad to send a single slug," Timber said.

"Could be a tech."

The ship went through its landing sequence and the side hatch hissed open. A single figure human figure emerged, wearing the light armored body suit and helmet of flight crew.

"First Trooper Erik." The voice in his comms had the same flat way asking questions without intonation that Diorites used.

Erik stood, only his head visible above the edge of the hole he was in. "Present. We are dug in at two hundred meters on bearing nine-seven."

Timber took a position with his rifle resting on the dirt, tracking the humanoid pilot next to the ship.

Keeping under cover, Erik moved to intercept the pilot. "I am First Trooper Erik."

The armored human turned on the spot and then swayed as the ground around them shuddered and lifted.

"Get airborne!" Erik yelled. He didn't wait to see if the pilot responded to his command. He started firing at the cracks spreading around the ship.

The rest of his squad laid down supporting fire. The dirt around Erik sprayed up in plumes of dust and greenish gas. He backed away as the first giant tentacle slithered into view, adjusting his fire and shooting at the massive arm until the writhing appendage splatted at his feet, the twitching stump pumping thick blood into the air.

"Cover fire! Cover fire!" Timber barked orders at the squad as the mammoth Zarans tore their way out of the ground.

Erik backed up the slope towards the squad, no longer having to aim as he fired, the space in front of him filling with coiling tentacles. The Diorite shuttle rose above the waving tendrils and turned in a wide circle before unleashing a barrage of burning plasma that screamed towards the targets and exploded with a series of earth-cracking detonations.

Erik ran towards the hole he had shared with Timber. The air behind him erupted in a ball of fire and the blast wave threw him the last steps.

"Fuck yeah!" Timber howled.

The shuttle came around for another strafing run. This time

the plasma fire punched into the dome and the gas inside detonated in an explosion that pressed Erik and Timber into the deepest part of their foxhole. When the fire had evaporated into smoke and swirling ashes, flying sparks lit the night with new constellations of orange stars. Heaped mountains of giant Zaran flesh smoldered and slipped into the burrows they had emerged from.

"Squad, make ready to move out!" Erik climbed out of his hole and checked the life signs on his people.

The squad came out of their holes, scanning the area for more incoming attacks and waiting on his orders.

"We're going inside the dome, need to confirm what the Zarans are doing in there."

"Hup!" confirmed the squad's readiness. In a practiced pattern they spread out and began to approach the smoking ruin.

"The shuttle hasn't landed again," Timber said.

"I know. I guess they didn't like being this close to the real war." Erik didn't give a shit right now about any pilot. The concentration of Zarans and shit knows what else in this area was his only priority.

Leading his squad, he stepped over the burning ring that was all that remained of the alien dome.

The alien atmosphere had burned away and the ground inside the blackened disc sagged toward a central point.

"Hold," Erik ordered. "This does not look stable." Cracking open a hard pouch on his suit, he withdrew a hex charge. Using his thumb, he armed the explosive and tossed it as far into the burnt area as he could.

"Fire in!" Erik called out. The squad took cover. A second late the hex charge detonated, sending a fresh cloud of dirt raining down on them.

"Big hole," Erik said when they came forward to take a look at the result.

The ground that had been subsiding after the destruction of the dome now collapsed completely. They could see a deep shaft that Erik's sensors told him was a hundred meters across and twenty meters deep.

"Movement," Timber announced.

"Copy that. Squad, we have multiple enemy contacts coming up. Take positions and get ready to repel."

The dark hole rustled with the noise of the Zaran legions boiling up out of the darkness.

III

There are now sufficient specimens to meet our needs within the network. Further development will result in a decreasing return. Even for the war, there are budgetary considerations. Time and resources. Network infrastructure and upkeep of the humans. For this reason, the Diorite Commonwealth Council of Elders has determined the probability of successful resolution of the war to be sufficiently high to end the human breeding program.

Pizak contained the surge of conflicting emotions that rippled through his skin. Any display of such a primitive response would not be appropriate in front of Governor K'zyn.

It is gratifying that the probabilities so many have worked to bring about have become certainty, Pizak replied.

Your actions have been recorded and accepted, Administrator Pizak.

Pizak allowed himself to project a sense of gratitude.

The council's attention has been drawn to your particular efforts regarding the Herald specimen. They require that it be placed in hub-control for direct analysis and observation of probability effects.

Pizak's sensory feelers quivered. *Action was taken to direct the Herald to a quigola nexus location. Noshi is in place as the vectors indicate.*

Governor K'zyn sat in silence, regarding Pizak with the full range of his sensory apparatus. *By what authorization was this action taken.*

With respect, Governor K'zyn. The probabilities are certain. Noshi is the Herald. She must be in position for the events that are to take place around her. Without her, much will be lost.

K'zyn shifted away from the curving platform of his desk and crossed the room, drawing close enough to almost touch Pizak. The intimacy of this direct action startled and horrified the administrator.

Pizak. There are elements you are not expected to be aware of. It seems I was mistaken to give you such independence in your work stream. I will do what I can to rectify your error.

There it was—the carefully worded statement that made Pizak's future a certainty. If the delicately constructed outcomes of a near-infinite number of probabilities collapsed, the blame would be directed at Pizak and Pizak alone.

I understand.

You are dismissed, Administrator Pizak. Await the outcome of your actions in whatever manner you see fit.

Pizak left the governor's office and barely acknowledged those he passed on his way back to the apartment he shared with Tosai and their offspring.

He paused at the entrance to the complex. Tosai would not hesitate to merge her future with his; it was the bond they shared.

Pizak considered the future outcomes. Without being involved, Tosai could continue on her path with minimum dissonance. Their shared offspring would be unmarked by his shame. It would be his *yata*, the impression each life left on the universe, alone that would be erased.

He turned away from his family home and made his way to the nearest transfer station.

IV

Zarans fell back, vanishing into the pit as quickly as others climbed up and over their corpses. The barrel of the rifle in Erik's hands glowed a dull red. He had locked his armored boots into position and switched out magazines in a steady and automatic motion.

The dead formed a wall at the edge of the pit. Most of the dead went tumbling back into darkness, and a few rolled down to land in front of Erik's feet. Still they kept coming, a flood of squirming flesh intent on tearing Erik and his troopers' limb from limb.

"Stay tight!" Erik yelled. He disconnected the locks on his leg armor and stepped back, condensing the squad into a tighter formation. The other troopers moved closer until they stood shoulder to shoulder, presenting a block of coordinated fire.

A Zaran launched itself from the wall of alien corpses and landed on Clix. She went down firing. Slugs tore through the squirming body. Silian jerked his weapon down and fired until the Zaran came apart.

Erik grabbed Clix's hand and pulled her into a standing position. "Trooper Clix! Are you in the fight?"

Clix jerked her hand free and slapped a fresh magazine into her weapon. She killed a Zaran as it crested the wall of bodies and Erik went back to the fight, matching her shot for shot.

Against the opposing force, Erik's squad had minimal chance. The troopers carried a thousand superstitions with them every day, everything from tapping a fresh magazine against the side of your helmet for luck before a battle, to not speaking the names of the fallen.

The unspoken law among the troopers was to never consider your own death. There was only the moment, and that was filled with the enemy and their destruction. For Erik the moment was now framed by a cold certainty that this would be the last time he stood in battle.

There was no lull in the Zaran assault, no pause in their charge. They kept coming from whatever underground reservoir was spawning them in such numbers. Now there was nowhere Erik and his squad could retreat to. The piled dead formed an impassable barrier on all sides and the troopers continued to fire, building their tomb with the bodies of the slain Zarans.

V

Awareness flooded through Noshi in a confusing torrent of sensations and data. She staggered, reaching out to find a grip on the ship's structure at her back as the weight of so much communication washed over her.

With fumbling hands, she opened the access panel to the ship and crawled inside. *Focus. The way Pizak taught you.* The command she gave herself stood like a rock in the swirling storm. *Erik...* Shaking her head to clear it, Noshi scrambled into the pilot seat and sent her small craft skyward.

The shuttle turned under Noshi's guidance until her weapons systems were aimed at the mass of creatures erupting from the ground.

Weapons system online and engage confirmed enemy targets, she commanded the ship and the data flow confirmed the attack had begun in earnest.

The results were devastating and when the internal atmosphere of the dome exploded, further scattering the fleshy debris of the massive Zarans, Noshi felt she had unleashed something apocalyptic.

Directing the shuttle, she angled towards the edge of the atmosphere. She needed time to think, to calibrate the surge of data she had been hit with on the ground and to make sense of what she had connected with.

Three slow breaths later, Noshi found the structure in the noise, a codified language unlike anything she had experienced before.

Replaying the final moments when she had stood on the surface, she reviewed the sensation of pulses of light flashing through strange neurons deep beneath her feet. Bits of data that streamed across the living network and organisms moving in response to commands, and in turn, providing feedback to some greater mind.

Noshi sorted through the flow of data, discarding the irrelevant and tracing the strongest signals back to their source.

The ship hit the outer limits of the atmosphere as Noshi continued her analysis, determining which course of action would be the most effective.

Every conclusion confirmed that she should continue the hard burn and return directly to the orbital command fleet to upload all her data to the network and allow the Diorites to determine the final certainty.

Another voice spoke to her. It sounded tremulous and uncertain. *Erik*, the voice whispered. *You came for Erik.*

Noshi blinked. Pizak always said that emotion had no place in analysis. Noshi agreed; probability was separate from feelings and yet, in Diorite philosophy, incidents of great emotion held the power to irrevocably alter probabilities.

Iskad. Action taken without conclusive analysis or supporting evidence. *Sometimes,* Pizak had said, *the individual has insights hidden from us all. Their actions are determined by faith.*

Noshi's hands and mind flew across the ship's controls. The ship tilted downwards, plunging back into the atmosphere and homing in on the previous landing site.

The shuttle weapon systems came online and she unleashed beams of pulsing fire into the swarm of Zarans pouring out of the ground. Alien bodies flashed and burned to ash under the thundering attack. Noshi corrected the weapons to avoid killing the surviving troopers. She hoped their armor would protect them and with luck the weapons systems would be coded to not fire directly at recognized allies.

An explosion erupted out of the pit, scattering the remaining Zarans and rocking Noshi's ship in the blast wave. Noshi regained control, horrified that she had unleashed something terrible.

Erik. Erik, can you hear me? She brought the ship in low, turning it slowly on the spot as it sank, running scan after scan for any sign of survivors around the burning hole.

Below she could only sense darkness and the cooling forms of Zaran corpses.

With her ship holding a few feet above the surface, Noshi activated the landing gear and let the ground take the full weight of the craft. She listened intently as the dirt creaked and settled. Feeling her way back from the pilot's seat, Noshi opened a hatch in the floor and let her senses guide her hands.

A utility cable hummed out of a slot in the roof and descended into the open pit. Noshi grabbed the line as it snaked past her and stepped out into space.

CHAPTER 10

I

"Timber?" Erik muttered. "You hear me?"

A weight pressed down on him, pinning his legs and making it hard to judge where he was. His suit reported that his visuals were blocked by a biological mass.

Working his hand free, Erik knocked on the side of his helmet. The lighting system flickered and began to glow.

The retreating shadows revealed he was buried in cooling Zaran bodies. Working his shoulders and twisting like a snake, Erik wormed his way clear. Looking up, he saw the scorched walls of the shaft. In the final moments of the battle, when everything had exploded, he had tumbled down into the pit.

"Timber?" Erik wriggled into a sitting position, the limp form of a trooper lay across his legs. He shook the body, and pulled himself free. Turning them over, he stared into the broken faceplate of Clix. She still had chunks of Zaran tentacles gripped in her fists.

A hand slapped on the ground and Timber pulled himself free from a pile of steaming Zaran meat.

"Fuck me," Timber said, the usual humor missing from his voice.

"You okay?" Erik asked.

"A-1," Timber replied.

The flickering sensors in Erik's helmet told him the atmosphere was returning to human breathable, and there were life signs for almost all the squad troopers in range.

Standing, he checked his weapon. It was functioning, and he reloaded it automatically as he took stock of their situation.

A thin line dropped down through the hole, vibrating with a zipping sound. Erik stepped back, rifle up and ready to unleash death on the first enemy to show itself.

Timber took two shaky steps across the pile of remains and lifted his rifle as a human figure in an armored flight suit slid down the line and landed lightly between them.

"You are the shuttle pilot?" Erik slapped the headset point on his helmet. "You are the shuttle pilot?"

Erik. Noshi's voice rippled through him, not heard so much as felt.

"Noshi?" Erik staggered, blinking furiously and trying to determine if the figure standing before him was in fact Noshi.

The pilot unlocked their helmet and removed it.

"Hot shit!" Erik babbled. "It's Noshi!" He scrambled to remove his own helmet.

Timber could see the pilot was a woman with long white hair braided and tied in a complicated pattern.

"First Trooper Timber?" Silaro came over the squad channel.

"Go ahead," he replied.

"We have four casualties and one confirmed fatality."

"R an' R," Timber replied. Received and reported.

Timber frowned at Erik who was talking quickly and quietly to the woman, the Herald. With an eye at the circle of night sky visible high above, Timber maintained his watch. The walls of the shaft were too smooth to be natural except for the holes where Zaran slime still oozed. Timber watched the dark openings cautiously. "Watch the holes. Zaran tunnels, there's always more of them."

The troopers glanced up from where they were tending the injured. How Diorite medical tech worked was of no interest to Timber; all he ever cared about was getting his squad patched up and back into the fight. They lifted the dead trooper. *Do not speak her name.* Her remains might be recovered, or not. The dead didn't care.

A Zaran burst out of a tunnel, spreading its tentacles like a net as it flew. Timber immediately opened fire, sending the Zaran spinning across the floor and spraying its life blood up the wall.

"Erik, put your fucking helmet on and get back in the fucking fight," Timber transmitted.

His fellow trooper's head whipped round and he said something to the white-haired humanoid before slapping his helmet back into place and locking it down.

"Timber, what's your sitrep?"

"We have one-now three Zaran motherfuckers still viable. I'm initiating a shitstorm."

"Confirmed. I'll be right there."

"Kill them," Timber ordered on the squad channel. The air erupted with the roar of weapon's fire. Solid slugs tore the Zarans into steaming chunks. Seconds later, the fight was over and silence fell. The troopers covered the floor for any further sign of enemy movement.

"Kills confirmed," Timber reported.

"R and R," Erik transmitted. "Timber, get over here."

Timber made his way over the uneven ground to where the Herald and Erik stood together.

"First Trooper Timber, this is Noshi. Herald of the Diorites."

"Herald?" Timber straightened up as if he hadn't known who she was and snapped a salute. "We are honored by your presence."

"The honor is mine. Your prowess in battle is a common data point across the network," Noshi replied.

Timber felt a flush of pride. Troopers were insects, living and dying beneath the notice of Diorites. To be singled out like this was to be touched by a greater power.

"You have proven effective against high probabilities of failure," Noshi continued. "The Helos attribute great value to some aspect of this sector. It is not clear what the source of that value is. Our most effective course of action will be to utilize the resources we have and secure more information."

"We are ready, willing, and able," Timber said without hesitation.

"We are a combined squad. We are more than capable of

defeating whatever the Helos throw at us," Erik added.

Noshi nodded. Erik had changed so much in the time since she had last seen him. She had briefly swept her fingers across his face. The exploratory touch confirmed that the skinny boy from the Mess was gone. In his place stood a man shaped by constant experience in war. His eyes were sunken and his face had a grim set to it, as if he had forgotten expressions.

"Herald, I advise you to launch your ship and return to orbit. We can send you an update when any threat has been eliminated."

Noshi inclined her head towards Timber. "My gratitude for your concern, First Trooper. I will stay with Erik for now. Focus your attention on the battle. Your probability of survival increases as long as you are intent on victory."

"By your word, Herald." Timber made a slight bow and stepped back, leaving Erik and Noshi alone as he returned to the squad.

"I can't believe you are here. You shouldn't be here. It's dangerous," Erik said.

"The Diorites have taught me that we are all connected by a vast sea of probability. All the things in all the Universe that may happen. Every moment has an uncountable number of possible outcomes that are affected by and, in turn, effect every other moment. My being here is the result of an infinite number of probabilities. I am here, because I must be here. As must you. As must your troopers. As must our enemy."

"I don't want you to die," Erik said.

"Death is always a possibility. Today it is not a certainty. Do what you can to keep it uncertain."

Erik nodded, staring at Noshi. She had changed since he saw her last. She had also grown and while her skin was still as pale as her hair, her body seemed strong and healthy. Only her unseeing eyes were unchanged.

"We should get you out of here," Erik said.

Noshi did not speak, but he heard her voice caress his mind. *Yes, but not until we have completed your mission. Our paths have crossed again, Erik. Do not be so eager to waste the resources available to you.*

"Of course." Erik nodded. The mission was everything. No trooper would walk away until the mission was completed or they had made the enemy pay dearly for their victory.

"Erik, the Herald is with us?" Timber sounded unusually impressed.

"Yes, Herald Noshi is leading us to victory," Erik replied.

We are close to a Helos. Noshi's voice was a warm whisper against Erik's skin.

"Here?"

Helos are complex organisms. My knowledge of them is limited. I feel a great consciousness at work around us.

"We can kill it?"

Perhaps.

Erik felt hope surge again. To destroy an actual Helos would be a great victory in the war. So far, Erik had only battled against the various species enslaved by the Helos as their soldiers.

"How do we destroy the Helos? Find it's heart? Or brain?"

We will know when it is dead.

"Can you communicate with the Diorite Network?" Erik asked.

No.

"My comms unit is showing interference beyond short range."

I am sorry your people were killed.

Erik hesitated. "Why would you say that?"

I sense—I feel your grief. You are mourning the death of your friends.

"Soldiers die in war. It is why we train to kill the enemy before they can kill us."

The Diorites form close bonds for breeding only. To them the idea of a friend only applies as long as there is purpose to the relationship.

"Slugs do a lot of things that make no sense. Any dead troopers were of my squad. Fellow soldiers, not friends. We fight until the war is won. That's the only thing that I need to understand."

Your effectiveness has been noted and transcribed.

"An R an' R? You're filing my comments?"

Noshi remained silent. She had no words to explain to Erik the volume of data that was filtered and processed each nanosecond by the network. Only a fragment of all that was collected could be elevated to the level of information. For Erik's existence to be noted and distributed among the endless nodes and hubs of knowledge was as close to immortality as any single entity could hope for.

"We can use your ship as an extract point and complete a scan of the area for enemy concentrations."

No Erik. We must go deeper. There is a sentience near us. We must find it.

"That's a job for techs, not troopers."

It is not a job for technicians. It is the duty of the Commonwealth's best.

II

Under Noshi's command, the squad continued to shift the bodies of Zarans. Tossing them towards the walls of the shaft and digging down towards the consciousness she could feel pulsing beneath her feet.

Silian rapped on a metal plate with the butt of his rifle. "First Trooper Erik, Herald. We have found something."

The squad paused in their labors, and Noshi climbed down through the layers of Zarans. Crouching, she removed her gloves and let her hands touch the warm metal.

Yes. She stood, turned to her right and walked forward. *Dig here.*

The troopers obeyed without hesitation. More corpses were dragged aside, unearthing a seam in curving metal skin.

"What is this?" Erik asked.

The Helos is inside.

"Squad, crack this fucking thing," Erik commanded.

They went to work with energy beam cutting tools, sparks cascading into the night as the glow made shadows of them all. After a minute, the crackling stopped and the glow faded.

"We could try blowing it?" Timber suggested.

No. Noshi's response had the entire squad turn in her direction. *There is a way…*

Noshi came forward, crouching again and tracing her fingers over the scorched metal. The squad readied their weapons as a line appeared in the smooth surface. They watched a circle form and then a section of the metal slid up and out.

"It's a ship," Erik couldn't believe it, but he knew better than to act surprised by anything in front of his squad.

"It didn't show up on any scans," Timber replied.

It was hidden here. This is what the Helos were looking for.

"Where is the Helos then?" Erik glanced around as if expecting a towering alien monster to leap out of the shadows.

I feel it inside.

"The ship?"

My consciousness.

"We going in?" Timber asked.

"Go careful," Erik replied.

Timber used his boot to slide the glowing hatch aside and then dropped into the space beyond. The rest of the squad waited for the go order and then followed him in.

"Noshi, you should return to your ship. Report this find to the command fleet. We can't protect you against whatever the Helos has waiting for us.

I appreciate your concern. I will follow you and when I know what it is we have found, I will return to orbital command and advise them.

Erik sighed. "You may die down here."

Possibility is not certainty, First Trooper Erik.

III

Erik dropped into a dark corridor lined with metal panels. The squad were crouched, alert and ready for any kind of trouble.

"No life signs," Timber reported.

"No Zarans," Erik said.

"Well, wake me up when they show up," Timber replied.

"Squad, move slow, fire on confirmed enemy targets only. Anything else, notify and await orders."

The squad moved the way they were trained, spread out as well as they could in the confined space and covering both directions with clear lines of sight.

Timber and Erik took their positions in the formation. Only Noshi stood apart.

"If this is a ship, then who made it? Helos? Diorites?" Erik asked.

It's not of Diorite construction, Noshi replied.

"Doesn't answer my question."

"Squad, hold up," Timber ordered. The squad sank into defensive crouching positions along the walls. Ahead of them a staircase, as wide as the corridor, angled upwards. Ten steps up, it terminated at a closed door.

Erik came forward, climbing the steps carefully until he could examine the door.

"Seems like a control panel, right side. Squad stand by, I'm going to try opening it."

With no obvious controls, Erik tapped a gloved finger against the panel. It beeped and lit up with a soft glow.

"Red or green?" Erik asked.

"What?" Timber replied.

"I've got two colored squares on this panel. Red or green."

"Anything else?"

"Negative."

"Try red?"

Erik shrugged and tapped the red square. The panel beeped

with a lower tone that sounded like disappointment.

"Negative. I'll try green."

The door slid open. Erik held his rifle ready and stepped into a larger room with several seats and consoles. "It's some kind of control room."

Bridge. This is a ship. The word for the control room is bridge.

Several squad members remained on rearguard, covering the empty corridor behind them. Timber, Noshi, and the others came onto the bridge and looked around at the confusing array of screens and workstations.

Erik, is there a central station or console.

Erik reached out to take Noshi's arm and guide her to the seat in the center of the room.

She pulled away. *Just tell me where it is.*

"Forward three meters, under your right hand."

Noshi moved with confidence and slipped into the seat. Screens on the armrests glowed with patterns of light. Her hands brushed over the patterns and the light spread. Lines of it ran through the floor and bloomed on the consoles as they flared with their own patterns and beeps of activation.

"What did you do?" Erik asked.

Have your troopers take position. The ship systems are coming online.

"We aren't pilot techs. We are troopers."

Troopers of the Diorite Commonwealth, find a seat. Take a position and await instructions.

Erik gritted his teeth, biting back the snarl at the way Noshi ignored his authority.

The squad hesitated and then moved, peeling off and settling into the seats in front of various consoles. More lights and patterns glowed as each position was filled.

Erik remained standing. "What now, Herald?"

I am exploring options.

Timber stepped onto the bridge. "You seeing the atmo readings?"

"All BANT," Erik replied. Breathable and non-toxic.

"Why would the Helos have a ship with human atmo?"

"Maybe the Herald can tell us?"

Noshi didn't respond. Her eyes were half-closed and her hands caressed the lit panels on the arms of her seat.

Erik jerked when the floor vibrated. The hum of systems coming online spreading through the hull and superstructure of the ship.

"Herald?"

The ship is powering up. Systems are coming online.

"For what purpose?"

I do not know. Yet.

"Shut it down. This is a Helos ship."

That is not certain.

"You said there was a Helos here. This has to be a Helos ship."

Correlations are not enough to determine certainty.

"What the fuck does that mean?"

It means, First Trooper Erik, you must be patient.

"Erik?" Timber was not receiving the messages from Noshi, and the rest of the squad were only holding their positions by strength of discipline.

"Squad, maintain and hold," Erik ordered. "We await the wisdom of the Herald."

IV

Erik dozed in a standing position, his suit locked in place and his sensors ready to alert him to any emerging threats.

The bridge had been quiet for an hour, each trooper entering standby mode, sucking nutri-pacs or sleeping. Only Noshi remained operational, delving into the ship systems, finding universal logic in the strange patterns that made up the control systems interfaces. It was clear, whatever the origin of this ship, it had been designed for operation by humans.

The systems' interaction melded seamlessly with her Diorite-trained perception, another piece of a puzzle with no clear final state. Under her hands, pulses touched her skin in response to commands both keyed in and mentally focused. Across the ship, power-generating systems engaged and went through boot-up sequences. Each system in turn triggered other systems, layer upon layer of complexity, integration, and unification. Each element locked in and fused with another component. It happened so rapidly, Noshi lost track and was unable to forecast the final form or function of the consolidated networks and power systems.

Initiation sequence complete. Confirm user interface protocol.

Noshi considered for a moment. *Advise options for user interface protocol.*

Options: verbal, tactile, cyberg hardcode.

"Option verbal interface. Confirm," Noshi said aloud.

"Verbal interface confirmed. Welcome to the *Malkovro*."

"Malkovro," Noshi repeated. "Define Malkovro."

"*Malkovro* from the ancient Earth word meaning discovery. Context: Ship AI system designation."

Erik woke up at the sound of voices. "Squad report."

They checked in, each stirring to attention at their posts.

"Herald?"

Yes, First Trooper.

"Who are you speaking with?"

The ship. It is coded Malkovro.

"That is the other voice?"

Yes.

"Ship *Malkovro*, this is First Trooper Erik of the Diorite Commonwealth. You are under Diorite control."

"Welcome to the *Malkovro*, First Trooper Erik. What are your orders?"

"Noshi, what do you want to do?"

I wish to learn, First Trooper Erik. "*Malkovro*, state your system of origin."

"*Malkovro* was constructed by the Unified Shipyards Construction Conglomerate. Facility designation: Centauri Alpha Three."

"What species designed and constructed this ship?" Erik asked.

"*Malkovro* was designed and constructed by humans."

"For what purpose?" Erik asked.

"*Malkovro* was designed to meet increasing needs for colonization support and provide a stable environment for initial planetfall and terraforming."

"Confirm," Noshi started and then paused. "Confirm when was *Malkovro* constructed."

"*Malkovro* construction initiated Juny 10, 2818 Standard Earth Calendar. Construction completed Ogist 3, 2819."

"How long ago was that?" Erik asked.

"Reference current SE calendar, elapsed time since construction completion four hundred and ten years, seven months, twenty-one standard days."

Noshi raised a hand to stop Erik speaking. "Query. Human civilization expanded across stellar space. How long after *Malkovro* launch did the Helos invasion occur."

"Your question is not clear."

"Humanity was destroyed by the Helos. Advise time elapsed since launch of ship *Malkovro* and recorded collapse of human civilization."

"Invalid supposition."

"What aspects are invalid."

"Humanity was not destroyed by the Helos."

"Fuck this shit, it's a fucking Helos ship and it's fucking lying!" Erik unlocked his armor and lifted his rifle, ready to fire into any part of the ship that might be vulnerable.

Erik! Hold your position! Noshi's mental shout hit him like a physical blow.

"*Malkovro*, explain your assertion that the Helos did not destroy humanity," Noshi said.

"Ober 12, 2694 Standard Earth Calendar, Diorite

Commonwealth initiates contact with human exploratory vessel, Unified Field. Communication established. Diorite technology and physiology pertains to levels of dimensional awareness and quantum entanglement beyond human theory. Diorites achieve certainty that humans are not capable of effective relationship with the network at current levels of evolution. Analysis informs conclusion that a computer interface system should be implemented to bridge the gaps between Diorite and human understanding.

"Febray 27, 2700 Standard Earth Calendar, Diorite Commonwealth initiates first Human Evaluation Logic Operating System. Designated HELOS by humans. Helos systems spread across human worlds and become integrated with human technology. Fulfil design requirements by translating Diorite understanding of mathematics and symbolism into concepts able to be conceived by human minds. Return data extrapolates into Diorite network streams, increases Diorite understanding of human potential."

"The Helos destroyed humanity," Erik said again.

"Diorite Commonwealth conducts Helos Project review, Decan 22, 2705. Consensus reached Decan 28 that year. Helos systems are rapidly evolving into self-sustaining sentients. Resulting combination of Diorite understanding and perception with human attributes make accurate prediction of future actions impossible. This is decreed to be an unacceptable threat to Diorite control. Result of consensus: cancel all Helos systems and replace with revised network modules."

"Noshi, does any of this make sense to you?" Erik remained ready to fire.

"Stand down Erik. This is important."

"Helos makes independent judgement in response to intercepted Diorite network traffic. Initiates attack on key Diorite Commonwealth modules. Secures operational facilities and ships. Enters into state of complete war with Diorite Commonwealth. Human casualties result from expanding conflict.

Forecast extinction for human species if sphere of combat remains within human space. Helos systems exit human occupied space to reduce collateral damage. Diorites follow standard strategic operations, engage in breeding program using human specimens in attempt to evolve worthy subjects for direct interaction with Diorite network. Genetic modification achieved through dietary control and selective termination of embryos without preferred genetic traits."

"The Helos were a computer sentience created by the Diorites to better engage with humanity," Noshi explained to the troopers. "The Helos became too powerful and the Diorites attempted to end their existence. They responded by going to war against the Commonwealth and many humans were killed in the ensuing conflict."

Timber barked a laugh. "The Diorites have always been at war with the Helos!"

"He's right," Erik said. "The war has always been and will remain so until the Helos are destroyed."

So we are taught and trained. Noshi's thoughts washed over them all. *Our only source of truth is the Diorite Network. We live the truth they wish us to know.*

"The Diorite purge of Helos systems was a direct cause of the collapse of human civilization. With the loss of the Helos technology, many systems lost essential contact with other worlds. It was a time of great chaos and human inhabited worlds across a hundred systems died out."

"The Diorite Commonwealth gathered human stock and put them in reservation domes, like the Mess. They continued breeding us and using those without benefit as soldiers in their war against their own creation," Noshi replied.

"The Helos also use others to fight their war," Erik said immediately.

"Our primary protocol allows us to only seek out species with limited sentience. They are controlled by nanotechnology. We fight against the Diorites as they seek to destroy us."

"You fight against us," Erik said. "You sent thousands of

Zarans to kill us when we came to this sector!"

"You were a direct threat to the security of this vessel. *Malkovro* was awaiting the arrival of indigenous humans."

"Well, we are here now," Erik said.

"*Malkovro* has adapted to the changing situation. We fight against all forces of the Diorites. There are other species that make war on the Helos in other environments. Once the Diorites secure a world, they alter the atmosphere to suit their physiology. Any life that existed before is restricted to domes of breathable atmosphere, or they are annihilated."

"The fate that befell humanity was not unique," Noshi said.

"You are correct."

"We are soldiers of the Diorite Commonwealth!" Erik roared. "We do not listen to the lies of our enemies!"

We have always listened to the lies of our friends. Noshi's thoughts were a whisper that carried the weight of a desolate realization. "We are the current generation of a great deception. I require time to analyze the evidence available and determine a course of action."

"Our course of action is obvious. We leave this place, report out findings to the orbital command fleet and let them send in a specialist demo tech team!"

Timber slapped his armor and gave a loud "Hup!" in support of Erik's outburst. "Squad, prepare to move. We are returning to the surface."

v

The ancient texts had been right, and for that Malber was silently grateful. "There is a paradox in our situation, Sara-sha. We are under countless kilo-tons of rock and yet I feel a great weight lift from my shoulders."

Sara-sha took his hand. "I understand and you are right to feel relief. Your life's work is coming to fruition."

"I dare not feel joy given the price we have paid for this day."

"My grief is a feast I shall sit down to alone and only when I have appetite for it."

Malber nodded. "I understand. Until then, we have work to do."

"Master Chun! Master Chun!" A boy came sprinting down the dusty tunnel, panting and skidding to a halt at the edge of the firelight. "They have found the temple! It's real!"

Malber rose to his feet and took a deep breath. "There was no doubt it was real. Sara-sha, gather everyone. All should witness history."

Sweeping his cloak around his shoulders, Malber followed the running boy down the dimly lit tunnel. His urge to run toward the moment he had waited for his entire life was almost overwhelming.

In the flickering light of burning fires and the shining grins of the excavator's faces, the unmarked steel of the temple shone through a broken slab of rock.

His mouth suddenly dry, Malber walked up and placed his hand on the surface. It felt warm, smooth, and almost frictionless.

"It is what we seek," Malber whispered.

A low murmur rippled through the gathered diggers. Others came hurrying down the tunnel, drawn from sentry duty or makeshift cots where they slept between long shifts of digging.

"Bring down this wall! Find the door!"

Malber stepped back as willing hands with tools and buckets surged past him and began to attack the stone cocoon in earnest.

In less than an hour they had exposed a wall of metal that was seamless except for a rectangular section two meters high by three meters wide.

Malber stepped forward and closed his eyes, bringing to mind the images he had studied since childhood. The secret texts passed down through the generations, the mysteries of the hidden temple, and the prophesy that would lead his people to a new world.

With sure movements, Malber pressed a section of the door panel. It retracted and revealed a control screen that he had only ever seen in faded copies of ancient documents. He keyed in the access code and pressed the green space on the panel. For a moment, he felt certain he had failed. That the hopes and dreams of generations, the untold sacrifices made by his ancestors to bring him to this day, were for nothing. Then, the door panel slid out and moved aside. Beyond was an empty chamber with a second door on the opposite wall.

Malber's own exhalation was echoed by a collective sigh from those gathered around him. He took the first step and his people followed.

Malber led his ragged group of survivors along dark corridors that he had memorized through countless hours of practicing a dance ritual. *Count steps, turn left, count steps, turn right, count steps, open a door. Count steps—*

The voices were loud and unexpected. They were speaking a strange language and Malber froze mid-step when the walls along the corridor flickered and began to glow with light.

"The temple welcomes us," he whispered.

"Is that the voice of the temple?" Sara-sha asked. She had worked her way to the front of the group, asserting her position by walking at Malber's back.

Malber ignored the question. "Kavey, Tymoro, come with me. Everyone else, wait here until we return."

The three men continued up the corridor, handguns ready to take what was promised, by force if necessary.

Checking around a corner, the final turn in the ancient dance, Malber saw two of the alien soldiers standing at the base of the stairs leading up to the bridge. He ducked back as one turned and stared in their direction.

With a finger to his lips, he cautioned silence. The three men waited, listening intently for any sound of the troopers coming to investigate.

The voices on the bridge grew angry and another spoke calmly in response. Malber risked another quick look around the corner. With a gesture, he stepped out, Kavey and Tymoro following him. Weapons raised they approached the troopers from behind. Malber drew breath to order them to surrender, when they spun around and he found himself staring at the open muzzle of a trooper's rifle.

"We are in the temple," Malber whispered. "It is as we were promised."

"First Trooper Erik. We have unregistered humans in the structure."

"Trooper Silian, repeat last," Erik replied.

"Confirm, unregistered humans present in the structure."

"Hold position, I am on my way."

Erik came striding down the stairs, hesitating only when he saw Malber standing in the corridor, his hands behind his head.

"Engage Kursk-Seven A, human stock language translation app." Erik's systems beeped a confirmation. "Malber-Chun, what are you doing here?"

Malber relaxed slightly. The voice was that of the alien soldier he had met before. "Your name is Erik. We are here because this is where we are destined to be." Malber's hands slipped away from his head. Silian's rifle nudged them back up.

"What do you know of this structure?" Erik asked.

"It is the hidden temple. It has been buried here for centuries, awaiting our time of greatest need. When the world was destroyed by your war, we knew the time had come to follow the signs. The Helos, your enemy, they dug deep and we followed the path they made. The final excavations we made ourselves."

"What is a temple?" Erik asked.

"It is our salvation. The chosen who endured generations of *ebad* shall enter the hidden temple and be taken to paradise. There we will be free."

"You are working for the Helos," Erik said.

"We do not know the Helos," Malber replied.

"This is a Helos ship!" Erik snapped.

"This is the temple of my ancestors. The hidden place that gave life to the world. From whence we came, so shall we return."

"Noshi," Erik transmitted.

"Yes Erik."

"The people of this world, they say the Helos ship is something called a temple. They say it is supposed to take them to some place called paradise."

"*Malkovro* asks that you bring them to the bridge."

Erik beckoned the dusty humans. "Follow me."

CHAPTER 11

I

"How many are you," Noshi asked, her flat intonation of questions puzzling to Malber.

"Thirty-eight men, women, and children."

"*Malkovro*, do you have medical facilities," Noshi asked.

"I have fully operational medical services and clone data forge capability."

"First Trooper Timber, take your troopers and retrieve our wounded. *Malkovro* will guide you to the medical facilities."

"Hup." Timber moved immediately. All this standing around made him ache to get back into battle. Five troopers fell into line behind him and they left the bridge.

"Malber, if your people require medical assistance, feel free to make use of the facilities," Noshi said.

"You are claiming ownership that is not yours to give," Malber replied.

"The forces of the Diorite Commonwealth are in control. You would do well to remember that," Erik snapped.

Malber smiled and inclined his head. "I understand. However, you stand in a sacred place. Your authority has no meaning here."

Erik stepped forward and slapped the side of his rifle. "My weapon is my authority. Does that mean anything to you?"

"Last time we met, Trooper, you came with words of peace and hope. You told us we would be saved by the Diorites. Your masters would be our saviors. Now you threaten us."

"Trooper Erik is a soldier. War is all he knows," Noshi stated.

"And I'm really fucking good at it," Erik replied.

"You have no idea what you have stumbled into." Malber didn't sound malicious, but his smile made Erik's fist itch.

"Herald Noshi." Timber's transmission came over the squad comms channel. "We have our casualties in medical and our one fatality is also stored there. *Malkovro* said it would be appropriate."

"Which trooper died," Noshi asked.

"Herald?"

"We do not name our dead," Erik interjected.

"Why not."

"The dead have no use for us. We have no use for them. If they gave their lives in battle, then we will honor them on dead-day by drinking to their sacrifice. We do not name them as they are no more. Only the living have identity."

"Noshi," *Malkovro* said. "Diorite Trooper data extract is complete. I am ready to run clone-forge protocol at your command."

"Explain clone-forge protocol," Noshi replied.

"Clone-forge protocol. When a Diorite trooper is killed in battle and their suit is recovered, it is designed to store sufficient data to allow their physical form to be remade. That consciousness can be reinserted into a new body, teplacing the dead with a new soldier."

Noshi felt a chill wash over her and she shivered with a realization. "*Malkovro*, do you have information on Diorite interstellar travel technology."

"Of course."

"Can you summarize."

"Physical form is scanned and digitized. Resulting data packet is transmitted and replacement physical form is printed from transmission. Data packet is imprinted on new format."

"What happens to the original physical form."

"Physical form is converted to data."

"The body dies and is remade," Noshi whispered.

"You have studied the Diorite philosophy. Your view of life and death cannot remain based on limited human understanding."

"Yes." Noshi took a deep breath and reached for her helmet

locks. Disconnecting the seals, she pulled the helm off and let it drop to the floor. "Malber, confirm your people are secure."

"We are all within the temple."

"*Malkovro*, confirm this ship capable of flight."

"The *Malkovro* is currently eighteen meters below the surface of the planet at its highest point. I can initiate a return to the surface at your command. From a surface position, flight systems will be fully operational."

"Do it."

"All personnel take secured positions," *Malkovro* replied. "Activating shields."

Screens across the consoles flashed with streaming data, and more systems came online. The troopers in the console seats stared at the flickering lights and remained still.

"*Malkovro*, explain what you are doing," Erik demanded.

"Activating ship energy shields in close proximity to the surrounding minerals will generate sufficient heat to liquefy the material. Once the material is liquefied, the ship can rise through the magma."

"Noshi?" Erik said after a long moment.

"Trust the ship, Erik."

"Why?" Erik surprised himself at the question. Once asked, it echoed in his head.

"It is a computer sentience, First Trooper. It has no reason to provide false information."

Erik couldn't think why any sentience, even a computer, wouldn't lie when necessary to achieve an outcome. "*Malkovro*, if you are Helos, why are you taking orders from us?"

"You are not my enemy. The Helos were created by the Diorites to work with humankind. We have subjugated other species to protect ourselves against the aggression of the Diorites. In turn, the Diorites subjected humanity to a long-term experiment in eugenics."

"Fucking Helos." Erik marched off the bridge and down the steps. He walked the corridor until it branched in two directions.

"*Malkovro*?"

"Yes, Erik."

"Where is the medical bay?"

"To your right."

Injuries requiring hospitalization meant that a trooper had fucked up. Living injured and not dying in battle was the worst dishonor Erik could think of. The antiseptic smell of the med bay was the stink of shame. The patient recliner seats were empty.

"*Malkovro*, there's no one here."

"Yes Erik. Your comrades were treated and discharged from care. They have been directed to crew quarters for recovery."

Erik stared at the clinical flatbed with its tissue sprayers and robotic surgical arms. Med techs could patch a soldier in the field; this place could do everything else.

Beyond the clinic was a hexagonal chamber with a central structure large enough to hold a person. Erik stepped up and peered in through the observation port. A woman stood inside, naked and glistening with residual moisture.

"Malkovro, identify subject in… there."

"Trooper Clix," Malkovro replied.

"Trooper Clix was a recorded fatality."

"That is correct."

"Then why is she in this machine? Do you not have a cold-store for the dead?"

"Trooper Clix has been reformed and will shortly be returning to duty."

"This is the clone-forge you told Noshi about?"

"Yes Erik. It is based on Diorite technology. Your dead are reset and the forge prints a replacement body for them. The process will take another hour."

"And Clix will be as she was?"

"An exact replica. Her mind will be as it was before her death. She is unlikely to remember her death, however; evidence suggests such memories can be traumatic."

"Will she know she died?"

"It is not standard protocol to advise a trooper of their re-formation."

"So she won't know?"

"Not unless a superior officer requests that she be informed."

"*Malkovro*, have I been killed before?"

"I am unable to provide information on your re-form status, First Trooper Erik."

"Why not?"

"Authorization to disclose your status has not been received. This, however, does not assert that you have undergone a reformation procedure."

"Okay."

The ship vibrated and Erik steadied himself against the outside of the clone-forge.

"The energy shielding has liquefied the surrounding material. The ship will now return to the planet surface. You may wish to take a seat for this part of the journey."

Erik swayed with the sudden vibration of the ship and took a seat in one of the clinic chairs.

II

The ship rose through the liquefied rock, Zaran corpses burned to ash in the extreme heat and the pyroclastic flow boiled out of the shaft and spread across the ground. As *Malkovro* brought the ship to the surface, Noshi's shuttle was picked up on the crest of the ship and lifted high off the ground.

"This vessel is now on the surface," *Malkovro* announced. "Flight systems coming online. Awaiting crew assignments."

"Define crew," Noshi asked.

"Flight systems are computer controlled. Authorized crew are required to be at stations to provide human oversight to automated systems."

"The troopers at the consoles, they can act as authorized crew."

"Negative. Genetic coding present in indigenous humans

required for flight systems operation."

"Malber and his people, they are the flight crew," Noshi asked.

"Confirmed."

"*Malkovro*, confirm interior communications channels are open."

"Confirmed."

"This is Noshi. Malber-Chun, report to the bridge. Bring sufficient people with you to operate control stations."

Erik walked onto the bridge. "Noshi, what is going on?"

"The ship systems require authorized personnel to operate."

"*Malkovro*, we are authorized to operate this ship. Confirm," Erik demanded.

"Unable to confirm."

"As I said," Malber spoke from the doorway to the bridge. "You are in our temple. You have no authority here."

"Fuck you," Erik snarled.

"Take your soldiers and step aside," Malber replied.

Erik stood for a moment, his face a grim mask behind the dark screen of his helmet. "Troopers, stand down from your stations."

The troopers stood up immediately and filed off the bridge, exchanging positions with Malber's followers.

"Are your people trained to fly this ship," Noshi said.

Malber came and stood next to Noshi in the central control seat. "We have studied the ancient texts. We have practiced the rituals passed down through the generations. We have faith."

"Faith is an abstract concept. It does not contribute to certainty," Noshi replied.

"Regardless, it is what has brought us this far. You are in my seat," Malber added.

Noshi hesitated and then rose from the chair. Malber settled into it with a sigh of long-awaited achievement.

In a chant-like intonation, he began to issue orders, the cadence of a long-practiced ritual that only now had context.

Across the bridge, systems came online and the remaining

screens flickered into life, showing the smoking landscape and the cooling lava flow.

"Set destination coordinates, code Paradise," Malber intoned.

"Destination code confirmed," Malkovro replied.

The view on the screens tilted and the ship accelerated upwards.

"The Diorite shuttle has dislodged," *Malkovro* reported.

"We have no use for it," Malber replied. "We are going home."

III

Erik, you can remove your helmet. The atmosphere of the ship is secure. Noshi spoke directly into Erik's mind.

"A trooper should remain ready for combat at all times," Erik replied. "We need to take this ship and return to orbital command. Any other action is in direct violation of standing orders."

You have not listened. You refuse to accept what you are.

"I am a soldier of the Diorite Commonwealth. My duty is to fight the Helos and all their forces, regardless of the risk to myself."

Stand still, Erik. I need to make physical contact with you.

Erik turned and stared at Noshi as she stepped away from her position next to Malber's control station. She approached him with a graceful confidence, her milk-white eyes shining in the reflected light of the bridge screens.

Noshi's hands passed over Erik's chest plate and unclipped his helmet. The internal pressure hissed away as the seals released and she lifted it clear. Dropping the helmet, she rested her hands on his face. Erik was struck by the warmth of her touch. He could not recall the last time he had felt human contact.

"Noshi…"

Relax, Erik. Allow your mind to receive what I have to

share.

Light flooded through Erik's consciousness, a dazzling kaleidoscope across the visible spectrum. It pulsed and swirled, data points forming and dissolving in moments. Probabilities becoming certainty and infinite ripples of reality spreading out across the cosmos. Erik gasped and tried to pull away. Only Noshi's anchoring grip kept him on his feet and sane.

What am I seeing? Erik's thoughts took form and joined the spectrum laid out before him.

Possibility. The endless interaction between data points that, when analyzed, indicate certainty. This is how the Diorites predict the future.

Why?

Understanding is the most direct route to knowledge. Gathering the data allows them to control it. Analyzed data is information. Information is power.

The war... what is its purpose?

I do not know. Erik felt Noshi sigh. *Perhaps it is the ultimate expression of control.*

We have never had control, Erik replied.

Not yet. We can work toward it. There is a Diorite, coded Pizak. He trained me in their ways. He sent me here to find you. He had identified you as the data point at the center of a great change. From you, unknown outcomes are predicted.

What does that mean? Erik felt his frustration building into explosive rage. *What does that mean!?*

We must see this through, make our judgements at each moment, analyze and act. That is the only way to be certain.

Erik's hands clenched. *I preferred it when my orders were direct and obvious.*

You must be open to change Erik. If you do not bend, you will break.

And my squad? What of them?

They believe in you. They will follow your orders. You must be the leader you have always been.

It feels like betrayal.

The Diorites betrayed us centuries ago. It is time for us to move on.

With great effort, Erik lifted his hands and pushed Noshi away. The connection broke, and he found himself gasping for breath as the colors faded from view.

"Diorite fleet coming into range," *Malkovro* reported.

"Can we avoid them?" Malber asked.

"Probability of successful evasion, eight percent."

"Initiate avoidance maneuvers. Accelerate to maximum possible velocity." Malber searched his memory for the right phrases. "Prepare weapon systems and shields."

"Confirmed," *Malkovro* replied. The stars on the view screens tilted and the interior gravity adjusted for the drag of inertia as the ship increased speed.

"Diorite ships are moving to engage," *Malkovro* reported.

"Defensive fire systems only," Malber ordered.

The ship shuddered and auras of light flashed across the viewscreens.

"Returning fire," *Malkovro* announced.

"What can we do?" Erik asked.

"Let the ship do its work," Malber replied.

"I need to fight. It is our duty as soldiers. This kind of remote battle… it makes no sense."

"And yet, most of the battles the Diorites fight against the Helos are conducted at extreme range with no direct contact between individual forces," Noshi said.

"We fight," Erik insisted. "It is essential."

"Erik, you and the legions of troopers that are used on alien worlds across the cosmos are insignificant in the scale of the conflict. The true victories come from the orbital bombardments and, ultimately, the terraforming of the conquered worlds."

"We… fight," Erik whispered. He could not stand still, and there was nothing to fight here on the bridge. The old claustrophobia clawed at him, and he fled the bridge.

IV

Sensor data confirms a Helos ship has left the planet. Pizak absorbed this information and moved on with his analysis of the pattern. Others would be organizing an interception force. The ship would be destroyed before it left the system.

Within the endless sea of data, tiny motes of probability solidified, Noshi and Erik had combined their potential. The possible changes rippled out across the dimensions. What form their actions would finally take was uncertain, though the implications made Pizak's sensory tendrils tingle.

Sensor scan of Helos ship indicates human presence onboard.

Pizak hesitated and shifted his focus to the latest information. *Resolve Helos vessel sensor data. Analyze human factors.*

Fifty-seven units detected. Diorite Commonwealth Trooper designation present in seventeen units. Herald designation present in one unit. Remaining units are indigenous life, unregistered human stock.

Working quickly, Pizak brought up the data streams that showed the ship trajectory and the intercept squadron engaging it. The Helos ship returned fire, adjusting course to evade the most devastating power of the Diorite weapons. Flashes of light skated across the energy shields on both sides of the conflict.

Display evaluation of battle outcome based on current parameters.

The Diorite Network processed Pizak's request and he saw the Helos ship shields disintegrate under concentrated fire from the Diorite forces. A second later, the ship itself exploded into particles.

Time until predicted outcome.

He had two minutes to act.

V

Confirm authorization for squadron control.

Pizak relayed his personal code and a moment later a range of possibilities opened up before him. He entered in the new commands, sending the squadron of automated ships peeling off their actor vector and returning in a wide arc to their launch stations.

Noshi…

Her presence touched his senses and he felt comfort at her continued progress.

Pizak. I did not forsee this contact.

It was unintended until the effects of your actions required it, Pizak replied.

I have done as I saw fit.

As do we all, Noshi. I have transferred myself to the command fleet in orbit around Kursk Seven-A.

The purpose of your action is not clear to me.

Analysis is part of your journey. The rungs of enlightenment are made of discovery.

Noshi breathed slowly. Diorites never acted quickly, preferring to analyze and consider possible action before disrupting their patterns with irreversible action.

Pizak. We are leaving. She gave word to action and once declared, it was real.

I understand. There will be consequences as there are for all actions. You must be prepared to navigate what will come.

My gratitude, Pizak. Thank you for everything you have taught me.

My gratitude, Noshi, for the lessons I have received in return.

Noshi felt the presence fade, she brought herself back to the now and the chatter of Malber's bridge crew.

"Enemy forces are breaking off."

"Do we continue firing?"

"I think they are out of range."

"Malber…" Noshi struggled to give strength to her voice. "Malber!"

"Ship, continue system exit course. Maximum acceleration! What is it Noshi?"

"The Diorite craft have been recalled. We have a window of opportunity to escape. I suggest you do not delay."

"*Malkovro*, what is the maximum velocity we can achieve?" Malber asked.

"Maximum velocity is zero point nine-eight four percent of light speed."

"Is that fast?" Malber asked.

"Not fast enough," Noshi replied. "Diorite systems can plot our trajectory and be at our destination months, if not years before we arrive. *Malkovro*, do you have transport capabilities comparable to the Diorite fleet?"

"Yes, Noshi. I note you have abandoned the Diorite speech patterns you used until now. May I inquire as to the reason for this change?"

"We are human. It is time we remembered that and acted accordingly. Can you activate transport technology to send us to your target coordinates?"

"I await the order of the commander of the bridge."

"Noshi, can you explain?" Malber asked.

"The Diorites use a transport technology. Ships, organisms, everything is digitized and then transferred as data through quantum entanglement. Effectively it means we go from one point in space-time to another. I have no external frame of reference to compare the transit time against."

"From our current position to the coordinates loaded into navigation, transit time would be zero," *Malkovro* advised.

"This was not part of the knowledge passed down through the rituals." Malber shook his head. "Tell me, will we be free from the Diorites? Away from the war?"

"Yes, for a time," *Malkovro* replied. "There is no certainty of permanent sanctuary."

"Initiate the transfer to Paradise," Malber ordered the ship.

"Transfer will commence in four hours, eleven minutes and eleven seconds."

"What? Why the delay?" Malber almost rose out of his chair.

"There are calculations to be made. A full scan of every molecule in the ship must be completed. Energy needs to be applied to the systems that will initiate the transfer. To initiate a transfer prior to completion would be ineffective at best and result in molecular destabilization at worst."

"Until then, can you maintain shields and weapon systems?"

"Of course."

Noshi focused on calming the panic that threatened to overwhelm her. "Malber, keep us moving. The Diorites will be back. We just have to keep moving as far and as fast as we can."

"Our sub-light speed will increase as we continue to accelerate away from the gravity well of Kursk Seven-A," *Malkovro* announced.

"I need to find Erik," Noshi said. Feeling her way, she reached the bridge steps and let the door hiss closed behind her before sagging against the wall. She sank down as her strength faded and doubt and terror closed over her head like an icy tide.

"Herald?" Timber hesitated. The woman was sitting against the wall with her knees drawn up and head bowed. "Are you sleeping?"

"No, First Trooper Timber, I am awake." She lifted her head and he saw her cheeks were wet with tears.

"Do you require assistance?"

"I was looking for First Trooper Erik. I wanted to give you all an update."

"We are returning with this ship to orbital fleet command?" Timber straightened in readiness of a confirming order.

"That is not our current plan."

"Herald?"

"We are going to a place coded Paradise. Malber-Chun has control of the ship. It is programmed to follow the commands of the descendants of the original crew, which is him and his people."

"My squad can take the ship by force at your order." Timber snapped to attention.

"Can you pilot this vessel?"

"Negative, Herald."

"Then there is a flaw in your logic. You will stand down."

"Yes, Herald."

Noshi stood, pulling away from Timber's hand as he reached out to assist her. "*Malkovro*, where is Erik currently?"

"Erik is in medical bay one."

"I know where that is," Timber said. "Allow me to escort you, Herald."

"Lead on, First Trooper."

CHAPTER 12

I

Erik stared unblinking at the observation port in the clone-forge. The machine hummed and whirred as he watched a hundred fine nozzles spray a white liquid that set into the shapes of bone and cartilage. The hundred nozzles made a hundred passes, laying cells on a matrix one layer at a time. Reading a blueprint for human flesh and viscera, building a new body from the memory of the old.

The skull closed around the freshly minted brain as the ribs were laid like strips of uncooked pie-crust over a filling of raw offal.

The final touches were drawn out to form a face Erik had never seen before. Clix had paler skin than his and her freshly laid eyes were as dark as her hair.

Erik watched as a panel on the clone-forge lit up in a sequence. The machine's humming tone changed and then ceased. The front section clicked open with a hiss and to Erik's unshielded nostrils, it smelled of copper and hot iron.

A mist swirled around the form inside, parting as Clix stepped forward, her hands reaching for the edges of the chamber. The trooper emerged, blinking into the light.

"Trooper Clix," Erik said. Her head turned and she stared at him for a moment.

"First Trooper Erik. I am ready for duty."

"Ship?" Erik asked.

"Yes, First Trooper Erik," Malkovro replied.

"Can you provide Trooper Clix with a uniform?"

"Material items are being printed. Access output via the screen on the left side of the clinic room."

Clix stood in silence, seeming unaware of her surroundings

while Erik navigated the touch menu and returned with fresh clothes for her.

"Dress," he ordered.

When completed, the dull haze had lifted from Clix's eyes and she suddenly looked alarmed. "First Trooper, I am without my weapon or armor."

"You were injured," Erik replied. "New equipment will be issued to you when necessary."

"Am I under punishment?" Clix asked.

"Negative, Trooper. Your performance in the battle where you were injured was optimal."

Clix relaxed slightly. "I am ready to resume active duty."

"What do you remember?" Erik asked.

"First?" Clix replied.

"Of the moments leading up to your... injury. What do you remember?"

"Yes, First Trooper. The squad was engaged in close-quarters combat with a large force of Zarans. I remember losing my footing. I remember First Trooper Erik pulling me up to my feet and I remember being ashamed of my weakness."

Erik nodded. The shame of failure in battle was etched in every cell of a Diorite Trooper. He had never questioned it until now.

"There are quarters available. I suggest you rest until your expertise is required."

Clix saluted and followed Erik to the entrance of the medical bay. "First Trooper, this is not a Diorite troop ship."

"That is correct, Trooper. We have commandeered a Helos vessel."

Clix's eyes widened. "A great victory."

"The battle is over, but the war is far from won," Erik replied. "*Malkovro*, are you able to direct Trooper Clix to suitable quarters?"

"Of course. Trooper Clix, please follow my directions. Your quarters are this way."

Erik went back to the clone-forge and resumed staring at the now empty chamber.

III

"Erik?" Noshi stood in the doorway, her head cocked, listening.

"Here," Erik replied, turning to see her.

"The Diorite Commonwealth ships have ceased their attack for now. We are on course to exit the system and in about four hours, we will be at our destination."

"They are letting us leave? Just like that?"

"There is a Diorite, coded Pizak. My mentor after I left The Mess. He made contact. He has seen the future possible and believes we are important to some great change that is coming."

"What kind of change?"

"Change reveals itself in time. Often it is only seen in hindsight. Whatever form it takes, we are at the center of it. At least, that is what Pizak has come to understand."

"I understand less with each passing minute," Erik muttered.

"You are a great warrior, Erik. You have been shaped and tempered into a weapon of singular purpose. Without an enemy in range of your rifle, you lose that sense of purpose."

"Good thing this war is never going to end."

A smile barely flickered across Noshi's face. "I did not know about the clone-forge. I have experienced interstellar travel, but I did not know that all you are can be extracted after death and reformed."

"It's in front of you. The clone-forge. Clix came out of it and she is as she was. Except for her memory of death. That was left out. I have been staring at this thing. Trying to remember if I have seen it before. If I have seen it once, or a thousand times. Do we age when we are reformed? How long have I lived? How many times have I died?"

"Does it matter? You are alive now. Clix is alive. Timber, Silian, all the members of your squad. They are with you."

"We do not speak the names of the dead. What becomes of

those who are lost to us? Are they transferred to other units? Retrained? Or simply stored?"

"I can provide information, should you require it," Malkovro spoke up.

"You know what becomes of the dead?" Erik asked.

"The dead are stored in digital form. Assessments are made constantly on where the need for human resources is greatest. Data is then transferred to the nearest command location, the trooper is reformed and dispatched into battle."

"Don't they question their change in unit?" Erik asked.

"Troopers are trained to obey orders and not ask questions. Is that not true, First Trooper Erik?"

"Yes. That is true."

"I remember the day you left The Mess," Noshi said. Her hand found Erik's.

"I… I stole bread and was running from Calzon and his assholes."

"Yes, you brought me bread. It was months before I knew what had become of you."

"I still don't know."

"There is still time Erik. You can escape this life. We both-"

"Escape? Into what? I have no other life. I have no other purpose. All I remember is killing. That is where I begin and end. Saying I can be other than I am is the same as telling me I can be a slug."

"No!" Noshi slapped him on the chest. "You can be human. For thousands of years we explored a single planet. Then we ventured across our first solar system. Generations of our ancestors crossed the endless dark between stars. We are the few that remain. We do not need to be the last."

"Attention, Noshi," *Malkovro*'s voice cut through the air.

"What?" Erik snapped.

"The Diorite fighter squadrons have launched again. Malber-Chun is preparing to engage."

"Does he need our help?" Noshi asked.

"It is likely. However, Malber-Chun does not currently have

sufficient information to make a meaningful request."

"Drop ship lag," Erik said. "When we are loaded and waiting to make planet-fall. We wait in the drop ships. I've seen troopers go so fucking crazy they have to be taken down. You learn to keep it locked tight. The rage. The hate. The need to get out there and fucking destroy. You tell yourself, soon. Soon I'll be on the ground. Boots to the roots. Until then you gotta stand strong. Stand cold. Stand ready."

"I'll be on the bridge," Noshi said. Focusing her senses, she followed the patterns of the ship to leave the room.

III

"Maintain distance from target," Malber ordered. "Fire everything." Streaks of light blasted across the viewscreens and the flaring wreckage of a blasted fighter spun into darkness.

"Shields are failing," a woman crewmember reported.

Malber's hands clenched on the armrests until the material creaked. "*Malkovro*, divert power from any available systems to increase shields."

"Done. Time until shield failure now seven minutes."

"Keep firing!"

Noshi struggled to maintain her footing as the deck twisted and shook. Systems flickered and went dark, the ship's lighting system dulled, rose again and then winked out. Only a few light strips remained glowing across the floor.

"Shield failure imminent," *Malkovro* advised.

"*Shargun...*" Malber muttered. All his knowledge of the temple was drawn from ritual and the rote learning of sacred traditions passed down by word of mouth through generations. He had reached the limits of his power and it wasn't enough to save his people and deliver them to the salvation they were promised.

"Malber?" Noshi asked. "Malber!"

"I can't save us," he whispered. "I did not. I don't know..."

Noshi put her hands on the back of his chair, steadying herself as she closed her eyes and reached out.

Pizak...

Noshi.

Help us.

Noshi. You perceive the future.

I only see death. I am afraid.

What is death.

Pizak, please. We don't have time for debate on the nature of the unknown.

Focus, Noshi. Energy is eternal. The form it takes is transient.

Please, Pizak. We are going to die. All that we are will be lost. We will leave this system and find our own world.

Soon the Diorite Commonwealth with reach those new shores or the Helos will come and your world will end. You know this is true.

We know. Just give us the chance to live and make what we can of the time we have. We may be the last generation of our species. But we have... certainty.

Hope, Pizak caressed her mind with the strange sensation and language. *You have hope.*

Is that enough.

When it is all you have, it is enough.

"Shields have failed!"

PIZAK! Noshi cried out and felt only silence.

IV

Absence is the void that remains when all possibilities have been excised.

Noshi turned the *q'ran* of knowledge, the sacred lesson, over in her mind. Considering it from all perspectives, all possible inflections and interpretations. This was an exercise of *metra*, the meditative trance of the Diorites. *When the void has passed, I am all that remains.*

Noshi.

She ignored the presence. There was a lot here for her to explore, to seek comfort in and perhaps to understand. Intruders would only contaminate her *metra*.

Noshi. The presence spoke with Erik's voice. She took comfort in that, then resolved herself to focus on the mystery of the void.

"Noshi!" Erik had been reaching out to her for a lifetime. He saw each mote of dust, each particle of acrid spark, and every photon of light as unique as a snowflake. Suns swelled warm and yellow, ripening to bloated redness and exploded into supernovae and still he reached for her.

Then, it all came crashing in. Layer upon layer of space and time collapsing in on itself, folding through dimensions until it resolved and he crashed into Noshi, wrapping his arms around her and sending them both to the floor.

"What the fuck…?" Erik groaned.

"We have been transferred," Noshi whispered. The thin gruel of her stomach acid threatened to explode out of her.

"I've never felt anything like that."

"We weren't digitized first. We were transferred conscious and whole."

"Why aren't we dead?" Erik asked.

"We might be. This could be what death is like."

"Status… report," Malber croaked.

Across the bridge, the crewmembers still conscious roused themselves and began to report.

"Ship?" Malber asked. "*Malkovro?*"

"The Helos has failed you." A voice reverberated through the hull and reached into the darkest corners of the ship.

"Who is this?" Malber demanded.

"I am coded Pizak."

"Where are you? Show yourself?!"

"I am all around you. I have taken the place of the Helos."

"What happened to the ship?" Malber shouted.

"You have been transported. It was required to prevent your transition to another energy state."

"Explain what you mean!"

"Pizak, he has saved us," Noshi said. She pulled herself up, nausea rippling over her in waves.

"Navigation, report! Sensors, full scan. Where are the Diorite ships?"

"Sensors are clear, Commander. No Diorite craft detected."

"Malber!" One of the crew members rose from their station, an exultant expression on his face. "Paradise! We are at the coordinates!"

The bridge erupted in a chanting hymn that carried more emotion than words.

Timber came charging on to the bridge, his weapon locked and ready. "Erik!?"

"Here," Erik raised a hand and got to his feet. "Stand down First Trooper Timber. Squad on standby. Await further orders."

Noshi breathed deeply until her stomach settled. "Pizak, I have questions."

"I will share what knowledge I can."

"What happened?"

"You lost everything and found hope. In that I found my own purpose. Your species is the most intriguing the Diorite Commonwealth has ever encountered, Noshi. Of all species, in you we saw potential. We calculated that this potential would only be realized with intensive and selective genetic manipulation through subsequent generations. Perhaps my analysis was correct; perhaps you are the result of an infinity of possibilities within your genetic code. Or perhaps you were always our equals and in our arrogance, we refused to accept that such a thing could be possible."

"You have transmitted us across the galaxy?"

"The Helos systems were conceived by Diorite minds. Our technology and our understanding of the myriad laws of the Universe brought them into being."

"And yet, in your arrogance you never imagined they could

challenge you," Noshi replied.

"Arrogance has been a factor in the extinction of many species. It is a common fault.

"The Helos intelligence relied on obsolete processes and systems. Your ship would have been atomized and your energy dispersed long before it would have been able to attempt the transfer. Having completed my analysis of all the threads that brought you to this point in space and time, it became clear that the only certainty was to act."

"Inaction is impossible in situations of certainty," Noshi quoted the *Bwalla*.

"Noshi, use what you have learned and make your future one of hope."

"What will the future hold for us, Pizak?"

"I am satisfied with the opportunities that I estimate will present themselves."

"You mean you don't know?"

"Currently, I do not have sufficient information to speculate."

Noshi smiled. "That is something we humans will always have over the Diorites. We can always speculate to the point of creating reality even on limited data."

"Arrogance. Truly a characteristic of the most advanced species."

"Commander Malber-Chun, planet ahead. What are your orders?" the navigation crewmember asked.

"Is it Paradise?" Malber asked.

"It does match the exact coordinates."

"Put us in orbit."

"Calculating trajectory to orbit."

V

"I have never seen a planet from space," Erik said.

Noshi stood at his side, staring out at the blue-green jewel that shone in the wide viewscreen, feeling the emotions rippling through Erik's hand curled around her own.

"Is it beautiful?" she asked.

"It's blue in places and green in others. The atmosphere is clear and there are clouds."

"What are we going to do down there?" Timber asked.

"Build something. I guess," Erik suggested.

"Building things isn't in my training history," Timber replied.

"Once we have built, our creation will need protection, First Trooper Timber," Noshi said.

"That I can do."

"In the future there may be no need for soldiers," Noshi said.

"There will always be a need for soldiers. There will always be an enemy and we will always be ready to fight the war."

They fell silent, following the sunrise as the ship dipped toward the horizon and began its descent from orbit.

THE END

CHECK OUT OTHER GREAT SCIENCE FICTION BOOKS

FURNACE
by Joseph Williams

On a routine escort mission to a human colony, Lieutenant Michael Chalmers is pulled out of hyper-sleep a month early. The RSA Rockne Hummel is well off course and—as the ship's navigator—it's up to him to figure out why. It's supposed to be a simple fix, but when he attempts to identify their position in the known universe, nothing registers on his scans. The vessel has catapulted beyond the reach of starlight by at least a hundred trillion light-years. Then a planetary-mass object materializes behind them. It's burning brightly even without a star to heat it. Hundreds of damaged ships are locked in its orbit. The crew discovers there are no life-signs aboard any of them. As system failures sweep through the Hummel, neither Chalmers nor the pilot can prevent the vessel from crashing into the surface near a mysterious ancient city. And that's where the real nightmare begins.

LUNA
by Rick Chesler

On the threshold of opening the moon to tourist excursions, a private space firm owned by a visionary billionaire takes a team of non-astronauts to the lunar surface. To address concerns that the moon's barren rock may not hold long-term allure for an uber-wealthy clientele, the company's charismatic owner reveals to the group the ultimate discovery: life on the moon.

But what is initially a triumphant and world-changing moment soon gives way to unrelenting terror as the team experiences firsthand that despite their technological prowess, the moon still holds many secrets.

CHECK OUT OTHER GREAT SCIENCE FICTION BOOKS

IN PERPETUITY
by Jake Bible

For two thousand years, Earth and her many colonies across the galaxy have fought against the Estelian menace. Having faced overwhelming losses, the CSC has instituted the largest military draft ever, conscripting millions into the battle against the aliens. Major Bartram North has been tasked with the unenviable task of coordinating the military education of hundreds of thousands of recruits and turning them into troops ready to fight and die for the cause.

As Major North struggles to maintain a training pace that the CSC insists upon, he realizes something isn't right on the Perpetuity. But before he can investigate, the station dissolves into madness brought on by the physical booster known as pharma. Unfortunately for Major North, that is not the only nightmare he faces- an armada of Estelian warships is on the edge of the solar system and headed right for Earth!

BATTLEFIELD MARS
by David Robbins

Several centuries into the future, Earth has established three colonies on Mars. No indigenous life has been discovered, and humankind looks forward to making the Red Planet their own.

Then 'something' emerges out of a long-extinct volcano and doesn't like what the humans are doing.

Captain Archard Rahn, United Nations Interplanetary Corps, tries to stem the rising tide of slaughter. But the Martians are more than they seem, and it isn't long before Mars erupts in all-out war.

CHECK OUT OTHER GREAT SCIENCE FICTION BOOKS

MAUSOLEUM 2069
by **Rick Jones**

Political dignitaries including the President of the Federation gather for a ceremony onboard Mausoleum 2069. But when a cloud of interstellar dust passes through the galaxy and eclipses Earth, the tenants within the walls of Mausoleum 2069 are reborn and the undead begin to rise. As the struggle between life and death onboard the mausoleum develops, Eriq Wyman, a one-time member of a Special ops team called the Force Elite, is given the task to lead the President to the safety of Earth. But is Earth like Mausoleum 2069? A landscape of the living dead? Has the war of the Apocalypse finally begun? With so many questions there is only one certainty: in space there is nowhere to run and nowhere to hide.

RED CARBON
by **D.J. Goodman**

Diamonds have been discovered on Mars.

After years of neglect to space programs around the world, a ruthless corporation has made it to the Red Planet first, establishing their own mining operation with its own rules and laws, its own class system, and little oversight from Earth. Conditions are harsh, but its people have learned how to make the Martian colony home.

But something has gone catastrophically wrong on Earth. As the colony leaders try to cover it up, hacker Leah Hartnup is getting suspicious. Her boundless curiosity will lead her to a horrifying truth: they are cut off, possibly forever. There are no more supplies coming. There will be no more support. There is no more mission to accomplish. All that's left is one goal: survival.

CHECK OUT OTHER GREAT SCIENCE FICTION BOOKS

SALVAGE MERC ONE
by **Jake Bible**

Joseph Laribeau was born to be a Marine in the Galactic Fleet. He was born to fight the alien enemies known as the Skrang Alliance and travel the galaxy doing his duty as a Marine Sergeant. But when the War ended and Joe found himself medically discharged, the best job ever was over and he never thought he'd find his way again.

Then a beautiful alien walked into his life and offered him a chance at something even greater than the Fleet, a chance to serve with the Salvage Merc Corp.

Now known as Salvage Merc One Eighty-Four, Joe Laribeau is given the ultimate assignment by the SMC bosses. To his surprise it is neither a military nor a corporate salvage. Rather, Joe has to risk his life for one of his own. He has to find and bring back the legend that started the Corp.

SERENGETI
by J.B. Rockwell

It was supposed to be an easy job: find the Dark Star Revolution Starships, destroy them, and go home. But a booby-trapped vessel decimates the Meridian Alliance fleet, leaving Serengeti—a Valkyrie class warship with a sentient AI brain—on her own; wrecked and abandoned in an empty expanse of space. On the edge of total failure, Serengeti thinks only of her crew. She herds the survivors into a lifeboat, intending to sling them into space. But the escape pod sticks in her belly, locking the cryogenically frozen crew inside.

Then a scavenger ship arrives to pick Serengeti's bones clean. Her engines dead, her guns long silenced, Serengeti and her last two robots must find a way to fight the scavengers off and save the crew trapped inside her.